DISORDER

propeller

DISORDER

stories
DAN DEWEESE

PROPELLER BOOKS
P.O. Box 1238
Portland, OR 97207

This book is a work of fiction. Names, characters, places, and incidents either are products of the author's imagination or are used fictitiously. Any resemblance to actual events or locales or persons, living or dead, is entirely coincidental.

Copyright © 2012 Dan DeWeese

All rights reserved. No part of this book may be used or reproduced in any manner whatsoever without written permission from the publisher, except in the case of brief quotations embodied in critical articles or reviews. For further information, contact Propeller Books,
P.O. Box 1238, Portland, OR 97207-1238.

First U.S. Edition 2012

Cover and interior design by Context

Published by Propeller Books, Portland, Oregon.
ISBN 978-0-9827704-2-9

These stories previously appeared in the following publications: "The Sleeper" in *Portland Noir*, 2009; "The Problem of the House" in *New England Review*, Summer 2003; "Peterson Wins Pritzker" in *Contrary*, Winter 2005; "Acacia Avenue" in *Tin House*, Winter 2008; "Continuity" in *Washington Square*, Winter 2006; and "Leviathan" in *Tin House*, Autumn 2010.

www.propellerbooks.com

Printed in the USA

CONTENTS

THE SLEEPER
11

THE PROBLEM OF THE HOUSE
33

ZERO
51

PETERSON WINS PRITZKER
85

ACACIA AVENUE
97

CONTINUITY
133

LEVIATHAN
143

THE SPIRAL
165

The Sleeper

1

At 2 a.m. I woke up and drove to the distribution station, a humid concrete bunker behind a rolling metal door just off a street of coffeehouses and boutiques in Northwest Portland which stood dark and empty at that hour. A thin layer of greasy newsprint ink covered every surface inside the station: it varnished the old wooden worktables to a dark sheen, fell in a sticky gauze over the obsolete headlines on the leftover newspapers stacked in the corners, and became waffle-shaped prints left by the deliverers' shoes and boots on the wooden stairs that rose to the loft level, where the manager sat behind a plywood desk with an old black phone. The ink also stained the deliverers' fingers, and showed as dark smudges on their faces where they wiped their foreheads or scratched their chins or cheeks, and it especially streaked the sink beneath the cracked and spattered mirror in the little bathroom where a roll of paper towels lay on the toilet in place of toilet paper.

2

The manager—wincing, pale, middle-aged, with tightly curled hair that rose into a ragged afro—looked down over the deliverers as they inserted ads, folded and slipped the papers into plastic bags, and stacked the bagged papers in shopping carts. He introduced himself as Carl, and pressed a piece of worn cardstock paper grimed with newsprint into my hand. Smeared fingerprints laced the edges of the card, surrounding the handwritten directions to my route. The delivery addresses were in large block letters, and between the addresses were smaller printed directives that mentioned which streets to turn on and how far to go until the next capital letters. Below us, deliverers pushed their loaded carts out the garage door to dump their papers into their sagging back seats or rusted truck beds, while others returning pushed their carts back into place so they could fill them again.

"You understand this is a seven-day-a-week job?" Carl asked. I said yes, I was fine with it. "I'm strapped tonight," he said. "Think you can try it on your own right off the bat?" I said I didn't see why not.

And so the first night was a disaster of missed addresses, cursing, and driving in circles.

3

Things got better after that, though. With every newspaper I threw those first weeks, I improved my accuracy and efficiency as I drove the deserted industrial streets of my route, slinging papers in a high arc over the roof of the car or flipping them backhand away from the driver's side.

I watched the papers slap against the scratched aluminum garage doors or bent black metal stairs at the backs of warehouses, watched papers skid across empty parking lots to hit curbs near walkways, sometimes tumbling to perfect stops against glass doors on which an all-caps *OFFICE* was stenciled in white. Once, after rocketing a paper up against the garage door of an auto parts warehouse and listening with satisfaction to the sharp report of news against metal, I made a tight turn and nearly ran over a huge deer that lay motionless in the middle of the empty lot. As I drove carefully around it, I saw that there was no head—the neck ended in a meaty stump, from which a thick black stream of blood ran downhill. Misting rain had collected on the deer's fur in pinpoint droplets that shone silver in the night, and I drove away thinking I should call someone to report it. I didn't, though, and when I returned to the warehouse the next night, the body was gone.

4

Two weeks later, at 3:30 in the morning, I saw the boy. It was only for a moment, through a screen door, from a distance. I was moving; he was in shadow. He looked three or four, but he was wearing a one-piece sleeper, the kind that zips from a toddler's ankle to his chin, so he was possibly younger. He stood behind the sagging mesh of the front screen door and looked out—at that time of night, he could only have been looking at his small dark lawn, and beyond the lawn my car, and within that car me, throwing a newspaper toward his house. Beyond my car was only the summer night, humid and pointless: a rusted freight train went about its rumbling business; a million insects hissed their muted roar. Beyond that, there was nothing.

5

A young woman doctor at a local clinic diagnosed my injury. Her high cheekbones, green eyes, and long strawberry-blonde hair were pleasant distractions as I sat shirtless on the paper-covered vinyl table, regretting my pale body. I recognized the woman—she'd treated my daughter Olivia just a year previously, after a bright red rash had blossomed across Olivia's face and her eyelids began to swell shut while my wife Sara and I played with her in the park. Unaware of the grotesque change in her appearance, Olivia had smiled when the doctor ruffled her wispy, translucent hair that day, and giggled as the woman laid fingertips against Olivia's chubby cheeks and smooth forehead. The doctor had proclaimed Olivia cute, told us the rash was a reaction to sunscreen, and prescribed a bath.

When I sat before the same woman a year later, Sara and Olivia were with Sara's parents in Seattle, and the doctor told me it was the first time she'd seen a repetitive motion injury from throwing papers. I received the news with a measure of pride. "You'll want to take a few days off," she said. "The joint needs rest." I explained the seven-day-a-week nature of my job, and she frowned at the wall behind me for a moment, then delivered a short lecture on the mechanics of throwing motions, followed by some demonstrations of stretches to do before and after delivering. "You should treat the job as if it's an athletic event, or things will just get worse," she said, and when she bent to write on her prescription pad, I imagined trailing my fingers down the curve of her lower back, imagined her skin soft and smooth and warm beneath her white medical coat and green blouse. She tore the sheet from her pad and handed it to me. "Talk to the other deliverers," she said. "See what kind of motion they use. If you don't change anything, you'll just be back here in two weeks."

6

I got the prescription filled at a grocery store and took one of the cylindrical blue pills with some water as soon as I got home. Then I walked around the house, awaiting dramatic effects. If I didn't go into my daughter's room and didn't open my wife's closet or any of her drawers in the bedroom, it was almost as if there had never been anyone else there. The dirty dishes in the sink were my dirty dishes. The clothes in the hamper were my clothes. The conceit dissolved in the basement, though, where there were other reminders. The dusty wind-up swing Olivia had fallen asleep in as a newborn lay abandoned in the corner next to her first playmat, with the fabric toys that dangled down: a felt star, a plastic ball, and a plush purple octopus the size of my palm. Occasionally I would catch the toys swaying a bit—a response to some phantom draft, I suppose. Or maybe the toys had their own vague, blunted intentions.

Other things that belonged to my daughter had disappeared: the plastic blocks she liked to scatter across the carpet, for instance, and her empty bottles on the kitchen counter, waiting to be cleaned of their formula slick. I thought about her little fists, the way she clung to my shirt when I picked her up, or how she bounced her palm against my cheek and then waved her arms and gave a surprised peal of laughter when I tossed her in the air. The nights were oddly still without the sound of her crying—that persistent, desperate wail of hunger, fear, or confusion. Sometimes, when I used to go in to pick her up in the night, she would shove her hand in my mouth, and I could feel her relax as the sharp nails of her chubby little fingers picked their way along the contours of my teeth.

After half an hour of pacing the rooms, I raised my arm experimentally—though the shoulder still ached, the shooting, knife-like pain was gone. The simple fact that the medication had done what it was supposed to do cheered me, and I slept soundly for the first time in weeks.

7

I was already particularly aware of that house, because the people there were always awake. When I reached it each night at 3:30, braked to a slow roll, and prepared to throw their paper, I often saw a male silhouette standing on the warped boards of the small wooden porch, shoulders hunched, moodily sucking a cigarette. When the figure was absent from the porch, he was certainly one of the people I saw through the front screen door, one of three or four men and women who sat on a low couch in a narrow room, their faces lit by an unseen television whose shifting blue light illuminated a haze of cigarette smoke. I didn't have many residential deliveries, and the ones I had were to properly dark, quiet houses. It bothered me not only that the people in that house saw me deliver their paper, but that I found myself unable to avoid looking in as I drove past. I wondered why they weren't asleep. What they did. Why they couldn't at least close the door.

8

I decided the distribution station was like hell: everyone was there for a reason, and most wanted to talk about it. A man in his forties told jokes about prostitutes and animals between explaining the complexities of paying child support for four children among three ex-wives. A doughy woman who sweated through the same purple sweatsuit every night and smelled of sour milk had three children in private school, though she cheerfully claimed to earn nearly as much delivering newspapers as her husband did selling men's ties. A man with wavy auburn hair and no teeth loaded his papers into a cardboard television box on a dolly tied to the back of his bicycle. As he pedaled off into the mist, the dolly's small black wheels bounced and rattled, and the bicycle's rear tire sent up a rooster tail of spray that glistened orange beneath the streetlights, then disappeared. An aging Deadhead with sunken cheeks, a voice like loose gravel, and spider web tattoos covering his elbows alluded to massive debt from years of substance abuse. His dog barked angrily from the back of his truck at anyone who walked past—its snarls were the last thing I heard before I drove off to handle my own route.

9

I took my painkillers with my coffee as I drove to the station, but the toughest part was when I first arrived and had to assemble two hundred papers before the pills kicked in. Bagging papers was dull, mindless work made even more difficult by the Deadhead's preference for tuning the small radio on his worktable to a station whose playlist seemed to have been culled exclusively from the soft rock soundtrack of my childhood: Cat Stevens continued exhorting people to board the peace train, Streisand and Gibb continued declaring they had nothing to be guilty of, and Joni Mitchell still wanted us to help her, she thought she was falling in love again. The deejay bragged about broadcasting these laments commercial free between midnight and three, and the Deadhead would play with the reception until he got it just right, and then tap his foot and nod his head while he hummed along. The love songs and the sentimental childhood memories they evoked in me, juxtaposed with the thuds of the stacked papers and grunts of the straining workers, made me feel my life had become the punchline of some arcane conceptual joke. After the Deadhead left to deliver, the remaining employees would talk about how they didn't like his music, but no one ever said anything to him. One night, after listening to Michael McDonald claim he kept forgetting we're not in love anymore, I decided somebody had to make a stand for sanity, and I asked if there was another station we could tune the radio to.

"You don't like this song?" the Deadhead said, incredulous. "That's the Doobie Brothers, man."

"I've heard this song five hundred times."

"It's the only station that comes in good. The others are fuzzed out because of all the metal in here, but I guess I can try—I don't want to annoy anyone." He started messing with the tuning, and for the next minute we heard nothing but static and garbled, distorted voices, until I had to tell him to forget it and just put it back where it was.

"Sorry, man," he said. "I didn't know it was a problem."

"Because you never asked," I said.

"Shit," he said. "You've been here a month? I've been here three years. Just relax."

"How am I supposed to relax when I'm constantly hearing all those shitty songs?"

"So I'll just turn it off."

No one said anything else. In the silence that followed, the sounds of everyone working were distracting and overloud. Even though I'd only said what everyone else was thinking, the silence felt like judgment. They considered me the bad guy, and I ended up wishing I'd never said anything in the first place.

10

Before she left, my wife claimed that she and I were driving each other crazy trapped in the house together all the time, and that with herself and the baby out of the way for a bit, I could apply all of my energy to my job search. Besides, she said, her parents would love to spend some time with their granddaughter. That I agreed with her when she said these things is not in dispute.

Olivia was starting to string together her first speculative, surreal statements at this time. *Daddy make a red roof house for Livvy*, she informed me on the telephone shortly after they left, and then repeated the phrase multiple times as if it held crucial information. Her sentences seemed crafted of some cryptic, dreamlike symbolism that begged analysis, and I turned the red roof house sentence over in my mind for three days until out of sheer desperation I asked the Deadhead what he thought of it. All he could tell me was that it was pentameter, which I thought would be interesting, until he explained what that meant. I told him I thought maybe Olivia had snatched the red roof house from some song on the radio, but when he started listing old songs with the word "house" in them, I knew we weren't going to solve it. And we didn't.

11

When my refills ran out, I decided to find a place where I could get some more. I chose a walk-in clinic in an old hospital in the rougher part of town, and waited my turn on the hard plastic lobby chair while next to me an old

Asian man sat with his head bowed and his eyes shut tight, absorbed with some internal difficulty. Across from me, a stocky man in overalls pressed a thick wad of blood-soaked paper towels to his forearm while he explained in detail what was unsafe about the motion he'd used with a box cutter; at the climax of his description, he lifted the paper towels to reveal the awful result. And there were at least three different exhausted mothers with small children who clung to their legs or lay on the thinly carpeted floors. The children whimpered quietly while streams of gray snot ran down over their bright red lips, and one stared at me suspiciously for upwards of ten minutes. Her eyes were dark, her lashes incredibly long. I smiled at her once, toward the beginning of the staring, but she didn't acknowledge it, didn't change expression.

When I was called in to talk to the pimply young doctor, I complained of back pain—too many hours in the car, I said. I also mentioned neck pain, from craning my head out the window. I felt these were plausible injuries, and found I could speak confidently when I concentrated on the part that was true. When I wanted to demonstrate my pain, I just tensed the muscles in my shoulder, which sent pain rocketing through the joint—pain I ascribed to my back and neck, areas I knew were difficult to diagnose with accuracy. The doctor absently picked at a pimple on his chin and asked me to rate my pain on a scale of one to ten. I decided my pain was an eight, a nine being burning to death, a ten, crucifixion. The doctor looked me over, shrugged, patted me on the back, and wrote me a prescription.

12

I kept pills in a vial in the console of my car as I drove past the warehouses and factories and stevedoring businesses that populated my route. I also drove a stretch of undivided highway, two lanes each way, and delivered papers on all of the narrow residential roads that branched off and weaved their way up into the hills outside the city proper. Whole strings of large homes hid within the dense green foliage of those hills, though all a person could see from the road were the rundown little houses on truncated dirt or gravel drives that branched from the side of the highway at random intervals. Those little houses with their peeling paint and rusted motorcycles and long, dirty weeds depressed me, especially when the car's headlights illuminated a small bicycle, soccer ball, or other toy abandoned in the weeds.

The house with the boy in the sleeper was one of those houses.

13

During the occasional phone calls I received from her, Sara updated me on places she had taken Olivia: Pike Place market one day, the aquarium another, and always the park. She claimed Olivia enjoyed Seattle, which annoyed me, because how can a two-year-old even know the difference between one city and another? And there were things *I* wanted to show Olivia, too—it's not as if I didn't see my share of animals or greenery. Hanging branches whipped past the windows of the car as I drove up a winding road to throw papers at the houses hidden in the hills. I watched opossums scurry along the roadside ahead of the car, and when they turned to stare into the headlights, their eyes flashed like silver discs. Jogging through an industrial park one night as I delivered papers to multiple businesses while the car idled in the lot, I stumbled upon two raccoons ransacking a garbage can. They spun to face me, annoyed by the interruption, and then, trading outraged bits of chatter, scampered grudgingly into the darkness. I saw plenty of squirrels and owls, too, and once even saw a wildcat dash into the roadside undergrowth. I thought Olivia would like to have heard about the animals, even if she wouldn't actually have been able to picture most of them, since the only animals she really knew were cats and dogs. But it wasn't something I would have been able to make her understand over the telephone.

14

What I thought would be Sara and Olivia's two week holiday had quickly become four, and then four became eight. On the telephone, Sara and I took turns telling each other the story of our life together. It turned out that though we were using the same characters, we were each telling a different story, and between our competing installments, we offered each other updates on events in the present. In Sara's story, for instance, I'd said I would do many things that I actually hadn't, so I seemed either deceitful, hapless, or both—and also, she and Olivia had found a playgroup right in Sara's parents' neighborhood. In my story, I was working like hell to pull through a tough time, but I was finding a conspicuous lack of support—I had also shaved five minutes off my record delivering time the previous night. In her story there was an entire thread devoted to thoughts on what love was and what it looked like and how it was demonstrated, and her parents had fixed up a room for her and Olivia to stay in. In my story the characters had definite goals, and it was important to establish what they each respectively and realistically wanted to get out of life and then to analyze whether the current situation was really going to help them achieve those goals, and also the last week had been so hot that I was sleeping in the basement. One thing our stories had in common were monologues devoted to doubts about whether the stories we were telling even raised the most important issues, and if not, what the most important issues might be, and if we couldn't figure out what the most important issues were, if it was possible that the important issues weren't even definable, that they were intangible and invisible but had real effects, like changes in atmospheric pressure or the erosion of stone. At the end of one particularly confusing evening of competing stories and traded theories, Sara said, "Well, at least Olivia's having a nice summer vacation."

15

A hazy, half-realized scene of my wife and daughter backing out of the drive in the car began repeating on a short loop in my memory. I couldn't even remember if I'd kissed Olivia before they left—I could just see her strapped securely in her carseat, looking at me as I waved to her through the side window. What remained clearest, the thing my memory rendered with the finest, most delicate detail, was the confused expression on Olivia's face. The memory didn't include the expression on my own face, of course—How could I see my own face?—and since children are such skilled mimics, maybe my daughter wasn't actually confused, but was simply mirroring what she saw in my own expression. Or maybe both of our expressions were authentic, and the same. It's a tough thing to unravel, the origin of an expression.

16

The next time I saw the boy, I was glancing through the

screen door as I always did, my eye scanning the bright rectangle of light. The adults were there as usual, smoking cigarettes and watching television, but standing at the door was the child in his sleeper, looking back at me.

As I drove away from the house and accelerated back onto the highway, I found myself so angry that I had to pull the car to the side of the road to try and compose myself. I stood on the gravel-covered shoulder and watched a freight train roll past until its whistle pierced the air for no apparent reason, and then I climbed back into the car and waited for a logging truck to go by. Its trailer was filled with the trunks of felled trees stacked eight or ten high—strings of wet, pendulous moss hung from the trunks, swaying heavily in the breeze as the truck roared away down the road. I pulled back onto the highway to resume my route, but the image of the boy in the doorway stayed with me. The night was one of the warmest of the summer, and though I was sweating profusely, I also felt chilled. I opened the vial in my console to retrieve another pill, but my fingertips found nothing, and I became confused, unable to decide whether the vial had simply gotten low without my noticing, or if I'd lost track and had accidentally taken too many pills. I felt jittery and anxious, and almost started laughing as I watched my hand shake when I reached to turn on the car's heater. By the time I threw my last paper a bitter nausea had risen in my stomach, as if my intestines had become entangled within some slowly winding gear.

17

I made it back to the station and into the bathroom in time to disgorge the contents of my stomach into the dirty toilet. After spitting the last of the humid brown stew from my mouth, I sat on the bathroom floor, my back against the wall. When I looked up a few minutes later, the Deadhead was standing in the doorway. "Your car's running," he said.

"I'll be out in a minute."

"You need anything?"

"I'm a little sick," I said. "If you could just leave me alone for a few minutes?"

I closed my eyes, but I could sense him standing there, studying me. "What's your problem?" he said.

"What's going on, Dale?" I heard Carl ask, and when I looked up he was standing next to the Deadhead, looking at me like I was an animal that had wandered into the station.

"He's sick."

"Is his route done?"

"It's done," I said.

"You can't spend the night here."

"I don't want to," I said. "I just need a minute."

Carl disappeared from the doorway, but the Deadhead, whose name was apparently Dale, remained. "Why are you even doing this?" he asked.

"Why are you bothering me now?" I said. "Why at this moment?"

"Because this is a shitty job I do because my life is fucked up. You walk around here like you're better than us, which makes you an asshole. But you're probably right. So what are you trying to prove?"

I hoped that if I ignored him he would go away, but he didn't.

"You should at least take better care of yourself," he said. "Especially since you have a kid."

"How do you know I have a kid?"

"You were just talking about her last night. Or can't you remember last night?"

"Listen," I said as carefully as possible, "I don't need your help right now."

"You just puked into that shitty little toilet and now you're laying on the floor, but you don't need help. I used to say shit like that, too."

"So then you probably know how much I wish you would leave."

"Have a nice day," he said.

I heard his footsteps recede, and I was alone again.

18

Later, I stood up, splashed some water on my face, and walked out into the empty station. An oscillating fan on a stand had been left on. It nodded back and forth as if speaking to someone it was unaware had left the room. When I stepped outside, my car was still sitting exactly where I'd left it, the radio on and the engine running. It was the only car in the lot.

19

The next time I talked to my daughter on the phone, she informed me that *Doggy make a walk with a flower sky flower*. When the phone was transferred to my wife, I asked if they'd gotten a dog now, too. "No, but we did buy flowers," she said. She was focused on her new job as a receptionist in a real estate office, and I was the only one of us, it seemed, who realized Olivia was delivering important information. I'm sure my wife didn't write out our daughter's sentences on notebook paper and study them the way I did, with a mix of pride and concern.

"You don't sound good," she told me.

"I'm just tired," I said. "I've been working a lot."

"Other than the newspapers?"

"No, the newspapers are every night. It's not easy."

"How long are you going to do that?"

"As long as I have to."

I heard her sigh, and could picture her expression, the way she pursed her lips when frustrated. "Why haven't you ever, even once, asked about coming up to visit us?"

My jaw tightened. I could feel the blood pounding in my head. "Are you trying to get me to?" I said.

"Don't start that," she said.

"We own a house here. This is where I live."

"I don't even know why you're saying that. What does that mean?"

"It means I have to work to pay bills, to pay the fucking mortgage."

"That's not what I meant, and you know it."

"So you don't know what I mean, and I don't know what you mean."

"I'm going to say goodbye now," she said. "Don't call me again tonight."

20

I was still rehashing that conversation when I got to the distribution station later and found a rubber-banded stack of white envelopes on my table. I asked what they were, and the woman in the purple sweatsuit said, "It's bill night. They should be in the order of your route. You just keep them next to you and slip them in right when you're about to throw the paper."

"That'll take forever," I said. "They're ruining our night

so they can save the price of a stamp?"

"They're penny-pinchers," the Deadhead said. "They don't give a rat's ass about us."

"You know what?" Carl yelled down from the loft. "I've had enough of listening to all of you bitch and moan. If you don't want to deliver the papers tonight with the goddamn bills in them the way they need to be and the way it's your job to do it, then you can just walk out the door right now. And you won't ever have to come back, because I'll replace you tomorrow with someone who'll shut up and do the work."

Nobody said anything. It was the second time that day I'd felt like a schoolboy being scolded, and it disgusted me that I could still be made to feel that way. I bagged my papers as fast as I could and left without saying a word.

21

I tried to sort through the bills and shove them into the papers while I drove between addresses, but it was almost impossible to mess with the papers while driving. I hated the fact that my route was taking so long, and I replayed both the phone conversation with my wife and Carl's challenge over and over in my head, savoring my anger. When I reached the boy's house, rolled to a stop, and looked through the screen door to see a woman holding the boy in one arm while she smoked a cigarette with her free hand, I slammed the car into park and got out. The gravel crunched beneath my shoes as I walked up the drive, but the woman had turned and walked deeper into the house as if she heard nothing. When I reached the door and knocked on the wooden frame, two men sitting on the couch inside—they might have been brothers—looked over in surprise. The one closest, who had a dark mustache and a thin strip of beard along his jawline, stood and came to the door. He wore a plain gray T-shirt and blue jeans that were turned up at the ankle above his bare feet, and as he came closer I could see that his hair hung to his shoulders in the back. "Can I help you?" he said through the screen.

"I've got a bill here," I said. "For your newspaper." He opened the door and I handed him the envelope.

"Who is he?" the man on the couch said.

"It's the newspaper boy, delivering the bill."

"Ask him if he wants a beer." The man on the couch raised his bottle as he returned his attention to the television. Though I was at an angle to the set, I recognized the images of a motocross race. Motorcycle after motorcycle flew into the air from behind a dirt hill, the riders in gear and helmets that made them appear only slightly less mechanical than the machines they rode.

"This isn't due right now, is it?" the man at the door asked.

"No, I just wanted to make sure you got it," I said. "A lot of people don't notice it in the bag."

The woman I'd seen earlier stepped back into the room. "Who is it?" she asked. Her cigarette was gone, but the boy was still curled in her arms. He was in his sleeper as always, and I could see that it was gray, with a pattern of small blue cars and red trucks. His head lay on the woman's shoulder as if he were ready to go to sleep there, but his brown eyes were open, and he looked at me with a combination of curiosity and fatigue. Both he and the woman were younger than I'd thought—the woman seemed in her early twenties, and the boy murmured unintelligible babble as he ducked his head further into the point between her shoulder and neck.

"The newspaper boy's dropping off the bill," the man said.

"Does he take checks?"

"We don't have to pay. He's just delivering it."

"We have the money, though," she said. "He's standing right there. I'll get the checkbook."

The woman left the room again, and the man looked at me uncertainly before opening the door a bit wider with his foot. "All right," he said. "You might as well come in."

I stepped inside and heard the screen door bang shut behind me. The man tore the bill open and examined it. "We don't even read it," he said.

"You're collecting money all night?" the man on the couch asked.

"No, I just saw you were awake."

"Aiming for a tip, huh?" he said, and laughed as if he'd made a tremendous joke.

22

The woman returned, holding a checkbook in the hand she wasn't using to hold the boy. She tried to press it open on the back of the couch, then stopped and leaned toward us. "Go with Daddy now," she whispered to the boy. He raised his head obediently and stretched his arms to the man at the door, who took him. The boy curled up on the man's shoulder the same way he'd been on the woman's.

"I've seen your son in the doorway sometimes when I deliver the paper. He's cute," I said. I reached to ruffle the boy's hair then, but the man twisted away, moving the boy just beyond my reach. Both of our movements had been automatic, I think, but my hand was left in the air in front of the boy and his father until I dropped it back to my side.

The man looked harder at me. "Sometimes he has a hard time sleeping," he said, and then, studying the bill, added: "And this isn't due today."

"It's not," I said.

"What's wrong?" the woman asked.

The man on the couch slapped his leg and laughed wildly. He pointed at the television, where a number of motorcycles were tangled on the ground and riders scrambled to pull themselves from the mess. "Always the same turn," he managed between laughs. "They always fuck up the same turn."

"How much is it?" the woman asked.

"We don't have to pay," the boy's father said, looking at me as if I'd claimed otherwise.

"But he's right here," the woman said.

"Take the baby and put him in his crib. He should be sleeping." The man's voice was tense, determined. He handed the child back to the surprised woman, who looked at me once more and then headed from the room, patting the boy's back and whispering to him. "What's your name?" the man asked.

"Travis," I told him.

"Listen, Travis. Next time you have a bill for us, just deliver it the same as you do to everyone else. I don't care if you see our light on, and I don't care if you see my son. Just throw the paper on the fucking lawn and move on. Understand?"

"I'm sorry," I said.

"I don't give a shit if you're sorry. You don't knock on our door in the middle of the night asking for money."

I nodded and closed the screen door behind me as I let myself out, then walked up the drive to my car. I didn't look back until I put the car in gear and pulled away. When I did, I saw the man still standing in the doorway, watching me leave.

23

My hands shook so badly as I made my deliveries to the next few houses that I could barely manage to get the bills into the bags, and when I pulled back onto the highway again and headed further north, I drove past the turn I was supposed to take. It was just a small access road that led down into the industrial area where I would deliver to a couple dozen more warehouses before being done for the day, but suddenly it was behind me and I was still going. It was easier to drive straight and fast on the highway instead of continuing to struggle with the newspapers, whose plastic bags snapped in the breeze that roared in the open window. After a few minutes, as an experiment, I dropped one of the papers out the window of the car and turned for a moment to watch it tumble crazily along the road behind me.

The sky was starting to brighten in the east, which meant I was way behind schedule. I knew that if I just kept going north, though, I would cross the Columbia River soon, and would be somewhere new when the sun rose. I pressed the gas to the floor, and the car strained to pick up speed. When I tossed the stack of bills out the window, I watched in the rearview mirror as they exploded into a mass of fluttering shadows, like a flock of birds in the night.

THE PROBLEM OF THE HOUSE

The problem of the house is the problem of the epoch. The equilibrium of society to-day depends upon it. Architecture has for its first duty, in this period of renewal, that of bringing about a revision of values, a revision of the constituent elements of the house.
—Le Corbusier, *Towards a New Architecture*

When my older brother Greg and I were small—I had just started school, which means Greg must have been in fourth grade—my father introduced us to what he called a "magic word." I remember it distinctly because he actually knelt down and looked us in the eye as he told us about it. My father was tall and thin, and his gray hair, coupled with the perfectly round lenses of his Corbu glasses, left no doubt that he was older than the fathers of my friends. I had never seen him kneel before that, and I never saw him kneel again after it. When he bent down to speak to us that day, I heard his knees creak and pop and watched him sway a bit, and I realized for the first time that there was a fragility to my father—that he was not, perhaps, physically invincible. I suppose his kneeling even frightened me a bit.

After steadying himself, my father explained that there would be times when, for our own safety, he would need both Greg and me to immediately stop what we were doing, remain in place, and listen to him for instructions. If we were in a crowd, for instance, and we became separated, my father said he would loudly say this magic word, and we should stay exactly where we were until he could gather us together again. If we were becoming too "rowdy"—a word he used often, to describe anything from obnoxious children to poorly designed buildings—or were wandering toward some unseen danger, he would say the word and then tell us to return to him, and we would be safe.

I told him I knew what the magic word should be. I said the magic word should be "freeze."

I'm sure my father had a more original word in mind than "freeze." He was extremely intelligent, with a large vocabulary that he didn't hesitate to use. He tried always to encourage us, however, and I remember him looking at me and saying, "Well, Sam, that's very practical of you. 'Freeze' is easy to say and easy to understand. I think it's a good idea: our magic word will be 'freeze.'" And so it was.

My father used the magic word twice that day to make sure we understood—once in the park and once in the grocery store. I remember that my brother and I interpreted the command in its strictest sense—we didn't just stop what we were doing, but actually froze like statues, our bowl cuts falling perfectly in place as I rested my hand on a box of sugar cereal and my brother's hand stayed twisted in my shirt, restraining me from grabbing a treat he knew we weren't allowed.

"Very good," my father said. "That's exactly it. Now leave the cereal and let's go. Your mother's waiting."

After that first day, however, my father's invocations of the magic word were few and far between. He made his living as an architect, designing buildings for a firm that spent the entirety of my youth attaching pristine, green-belted office parks to the freeway that raced through the empty brown plains outside of town. On the few occasions that I actually did become separated from my family in a crowd, it was actually Greg who managed to keep track of me. I can remember a specific trip to a Broncos game in which I lost track of my father and brother in the sea of orange shirts and jackets shuffling along the concourse in Mile High Stadium. I couldn't see anything but swinging arms and scissoring legs that forced me farther and farther off course, and I was about to panic and yell when I felt a hand grab the collar of my jacket. It was Greg, and he half-guided/half-dragged me back to my father in time for him to look down from his inspection of the steel girders overhead and say, "Looks like they made a real rat's nest of the upper-deck support here, boys. You couldn't make it rowdier with your eyes closed."

That kind of distraction on the part of my father wasn't an isolated incident. He was fascinated by what he did for a living, and maintained an admiration for Le Corbusier that bordered on the unnatural. We lived in a suburban housing developments in which, save for minor cosmetic concerns or differences in fixtures, each house was the same. Yet my father would often wander slowly through the rooms as if he had never been there before, examining doors or pieces of furniture or even our left-behind shoes on the floor.

"Dad, what are you doing?" Greg asked him once. "You're freaking me out."

"I'm thinking about the problem of the house," my father said.

Greg and I fell silent. I wondered which of us was the problem.

"I'm thinking about how our windows work," my father said. "Do you like the television in front of the window there? Wouldn't it be better in the other corner?"

"The power cord for the Atari doesn't reach from the other corner," Greg said.

"Why do we have these folding doors on this room?" my father continued. "This is a public space. Shouldn't we just leave this doorway open?"

"I want those doors there!" my mother called from somewhere down the hall. She was frighteningly adept at monitoring conversations taking place in other rooms. "The video game noise gives me a headache!"

My father thought for a moment. "We should establish standards," he said, and then wandered off to inspect other rooms. He was given to non sequiturs like that, especially on occasions when it was clear his mind was far more occupied with theories of architecture and design than with making conversation about Space Invaders.

The magic word lay fallow for years, unused. I didn't forget about it, though, and Greg didn't, either. It was frozen within us, waiting.

When I was in seventh grade I began to study French. This excited my father greatly—he felt it would be a wonderful exercise for me to begin reading Le Corbusier in its original form, so he ordered me a French copy of *Towards a New Architecture*, assuring me that it was written in simple, straightforward language, and I would have no problem with it. The day it arrived in the mail he eagerly opened the box and handed the book to me, asking me to read some of it aloud.

I took one look at it and told him no way.

Three months later, however, I managed to write out a translation of one of the simpler sections:

> Mass production is based on analysis and experiment.
> Industry on the grand scale must occupy itself with building and establish the elements of the house on a mass-production basis.
> We must create the mass-production spirit.
> The spirit of constructing mass-production houses.
> The spirit of living in mass-production houses.
> The spirit of conceiving mass-production houses.

I brought my translation to my father. He spent most of his evenings perched in front of an immense white drafting board in his study, painstakingly designing increasingly large office buildings and their attendant parking structures. He took a look at my translation and proudly told me it was perfect. I remember asking him why, if he liked this stuff and it was all about houses, he didn't design houses instead of office buildings.

"That's a good question," he said. "And a fair one. I think, Sam, that the reason might be that I'm attracted to the cut-and-dry utility of commercial projects." He went on to discuss the concept of blank slates versus found or impacted environments, the problematic multiplication of vision in serially owned structures, and other things that I had absolutely no understanding of and which, quite frankly, bored me. It wouldn't be until years after his death that my mother would explain to me that my father's flights into architectural theory were usually nothing more than his method of avoiding answering questions.

Though I decided I wouldn't show my father any more translations, I continued reading the Le Corbusier book. "If we eliminate from our hearts and minds all dead concepts in regard to the houses and look at the question from a critical and objective point of view," Le Corbusier wrote, "we shall arrive at the 'House-Machine,' the mass-production house, healthy (and morally so too) and beautiful in the same way that the working tools and instruments which accompany our existence are beautiful." There was an earnestness to Le Corbusier's pursuit of perfection that I found appealing, and I started carrying the book around in my backpack with me, opening it to random pages whenever I had some time to kill, which was fairly often in those days of confusing, rapidly changing junior-high cliques and fads. It seemed that Greg was similarly ill at ease with the high school social scene, and I often reminded myself that whatever happened in the halls at school, I would have Greg to talk to and hang out with at home, to throw darts and drink Pepsi with, to play ping-pong or Pac-Man against.

Around the same time that I was studying French and reading Le Corbusier, however, Greg began to change. All teenagers go through difficulties—and if Greg was anything then, he was a teenager, with the acne and breaking voice to prove it—but Greg's difficulties seemed more dramatic. He was angry, really—far angrier than any of the other kids I knew, so angry that I think even my parents were a bit scared of him. He withdrew almost completely from our family life, no longer going on errands with us, refusing to attend any of my seventh-grade basketball games (for which I can hardly blame him—I was allowed to play only during meaningless final minutes of blowouts), often disappearing for hours at a time. When he was home, he was in his locked room, unresponsive to all but the most urgent and authoritative knocks. He let his hair get long and curly on top, and then one day he came home with it dyed black and straightened so that it hung in his face. I knew things between us had changed for the worse when I found his room unoccupied one day and wandered in to look at his music collection, mostly a bunch of tapes by The Smiths and The Cure and New Order and The Dead Kennedys. When he returned and found me looking at his stuff, his face got bright red and he pinned me to the floor, punching me over and over again on the arm while spitting out a demand that I tell him exactly what I'd looked at while he was gone. After he was satisfied that I'd seen nothing more than a few tapes with unusual cover art, he let me go. I quit the basketball team rather than let anyone see the resulting massive blue and purple bruise on my shoulder, and though Greg apologized a few days later, I started keeping my distance.

The next fall, on one of the few family outings Greg joined during those years, my father finally used the magic word again. After a picnic lunch of ham sandwiches, potato chips, pickles, and soda, the four of us set out on a hike. As usual, Greg stayed apart from us, clomping ahead in his long jeans and black boots and moving out of sight on the thin dry path that wound steeply up the side of the hill.

"Someone's definitely in a hurry," my mom said.

"God forbid he actually talk to us," my father added, and I felt proud to be by their side, the good son that walked and talked with them and wasn't angry at the world.

After a short period of hiking, we moved around a twist in the trail and started up a long rise when we saw Greg about fifty yards ahead, coming back down toward us. "That's it," he shouted to us. "I'm done."

"You already got to the lake?" my father asked. It was a dumb question, because the lake was still fifteen minutes away.

"I'm not going," Greg shouted. "This is boring and stupid. I twisted my ankle."

"It'll be worth it," my father said. "Stay with us."

"Did you not hear what I said? I fucking twisted my ankle!" Greg yelled. It was the equivalent of a slap in the face—nobody in our family cursed, and I'd never heard anyone, anywhere, speak to my father that way.

"Greg!" my father yelled. "Freeze!"

"I'm not fucking freezing!" Greg yelled back. He was still stomping toward us, only about twenty yards away.

"Goddammit Gregory freeze right now!" my father yelled. My father's curse was another first, and enough of a shock to stop Greg in his tracks.

It was then that I saw something wavering at the edge of the shadows on the path in front of Greg. At first I thought it was either a stick or a piece of trash tumbling in the breeze. Then I realized it was a snake.

Though our science teachers dutifully informed us every year that there were rattlesnakes in Colorado, the only place I'd ever seen one had been safely behind glass at the zoo. This one lay in the path, separating my brother from the rest of us. The snake displayed none of the threatening behaviors favored by movie and nightmare snakes—it didn't rear up like a cobra, didn't bare its fangs, didn't slither rapidly toward its victim. It just lay there, piled in a flaccid coil. It rattled its tail in a way that seemed nervous.

Greg stared at the snake. Even from a distance, I could see his hands shaking.

"Don't move," my father said.

Nobody moved.

"Do something!" my mother whispered, though I wasn't sure who she was talking to—my father, Greg, or the snake.

"Don't move, Greg," my father repeated. "Just stay still."

"I want to run," Greg said.

"Don't run," my father said. "Just wait."

The snake sat there. It was probably three feet from Greg's foot. It rattled again.

"Very slowly, Greg, just step back," my father said. "Slowly."

Greg lifted one foot and moved it slowly backward, keeping his eyes on the snake. He shifted his weight to the back foot and half turned, leaning away.

The strike was so quick that I didn't see it. I saw a puff of dust and heard both Greg and my mother scream, and then I saw Greg lift his foot, and the snake was hanging from his boot. My father ran toward him and Greg kicked his foot, but the snake's fangs were caught. It writhed in the air and whipped its bottom half in the dust while my mother screamed again, and then the snake fell. By the time my father got to Greg the snake was gone off the side of the path, and when he leaned over to grab Greg's foot, Greg hit him with an open hand behind his ear and knocked him down, sending his glasses flying into the dirt. Greg tore his boot off his foot without even unlacing it and threw it away from him and started yelling, "Motherfucker, motherfucker!" over and over. My mother got to him and grabbed him and he fell, pulling her down on top of him, but she got to her knees and grabbed his foot and pulled off his sock and started looking at his foot and ankle. I ran to them and didn't even realize I had Greg's boot until my father ripped it out of my hand and looked first at the outside of it and then at the inside and then said, "No it didn't, *no it didn't!*"

"What?" my mother yelled. There was dirt in her hair and her flushed cheeks were wet with tears.

"It didn't go through the boot. The bite didn't go through the leather," my father said. My mother turned back to Greg's foot and started kneading the skin with her thumbs, working them across the surface. She and Greg spent five frantic seconds examining every inch of his foot and ankle until they were sure my father was right, and then my mother hugged Greg while he cried, and the crying turned to sobbing, and my mother sat there in the dirt with him, holding him while he sobbed, while my father held his broken glasses in one hand and Greg's boot in the other and I stood there shaking and wanting to throw up.

That was it for the magic word.

Unfortunately, that wasn't it for Greg's problems. The snake may have failed to poison Greg, but something about the event remained unsettling. I don't know if Greg blamed my father for making him stand still when he'd wanted to run, or if my father felt that Greg would have avoided trouble if he'd simply stayed with us, but the snake's strike was never really brought up again after that day. The fact that it wasn't spoken of injected an odd silence into our home, as if we had all decided it would be best not to risk too much conversation, lest some taboo subject arise. So we all went about our business, negotiating that silence as if it were simply an unnecessary wall or dead-end hall built into the house, an inconvenience we avoided or stepped around because to do so was far easier than undertaking a serious remodeling project.

Then my Le Corbusier book disappeared. Because I carried it with me so often, there were any number of possible places I could have left it, but I felt fairly certain that it had been taken from my room. I remember going to talk to my mother about it and finding her in the kitchen, her hair pulled back into a ponytail to keep it out of her face while she chopped vegetables for soup. She was an excellent cook, and I watched her work for a bit, mesmerized by the confidence of her movements with the knife as she took only a minute to reduce two tomatoes and an onion to bits. She began chopping a red bell pepper next, the blade striking the cutting board over and over again with the same rapid, precise rhythm that never ceased to amaze me, no matter how many times I'd seen her do it before. Before I could mention my stolen book, though, she stopped chopping, and frowned at the cutting board. "That's funny," she said.

"What?" I asked.

"I just sliced a tiny bit off the tip of my finger," she said. "But I don't feel a thing."

Sure enough, a small moon-shaped crimson stain was spreading from where my mother's middle finger rested on the yellowed wooden cutting board, and a thin white piece of neatly sliced flesh lay next to the last bit of red pepper. I ran to get her a bandage, then cleaned the board and finished chopping the pepper myself. I didn't mention my missing book.

Steeling myself, I followed Greg into his room a few days later and asked him about it directly. "Oh, is this the book you mean?" he responded, pulling my book out from under a stack of music magazines he kept by his bed. "This little French faggot architecture book?"

"Yes," I said.

"What's the deal with this book?" he asked. "Why do you carry this thing around with you everywhere? Trying to rack up brownie points with the old man?"

"No."

"What's this say?" he asked, opening the book to one of the pages I'd marked and holding it up to me.

"*Everybody dreams of sheltering himself in a sure and permanent home of his own,*" I read. "*This dream, because it is impossible in the existing state of things, is…incapable of realization and provokes an actual state of sentimental hysteria.*"

"Well aren't you a little prodigy," he said. Then he tore out the page I'd been reading, crumpled it into a ball, and threw it toward the trash can in the corner of his room. "What's this one say?" he asked, indicating the next page.

"*We are dealing with an urgent problem of our epoch,*" I read. "*No, with* the *problem of our epoch.*"

He tore that page out, too, crumpled it, and threw it where he'd thrown the first one. "This one," he demanded, holding up the next page. "What does that say?"

I felt strangely serene. "It says *Architecture or Revolution,*" I told him.

He tore it out. Then, with deliberate concentration, he tore the book in half down the spine. "This family," he said, "has problems. All of you, you all have serious problems." He picked up the halves and tore each of them again down the spine. "I'm doing this for your own good, Sam. I'm trying to help you." I said nothing while he continued destroying the book, tearing out chunks of pages and tossing them toward his trash can. He continued until he had dismantled the entire book, then looked at me and said, "How do you feel?"

"Why did you do that?" I asked.

He shrugged. "Because I'm not like you," he said. "I'm not like this family, and I think that book is a bunch of bullshit and I hate that you carry it around like it's your fucking bible."

"So what are you like?"

"Do me a favor, Sam," he said. "Don't ever come back in my room again. You're a kiss-ass piece of shit and I don't want you to bother me anymore."

There is something powerful about the idea of preserving a union, I think, and I believe it was that power and that power alone—the desire to preserve our family with all of its members intact, regardless of what that required—that sustained Greg's continued presence in our home over the next year. He never apologized about destroying my book or even mentioned it again. I would be lying to say that he and I didn't have any fairly normal interactions after that—we played darts a few more times, and even played a few video games until the Atari finally broke for good and my father threw it away. But Greg was absent more and more often, as well. He had a driver's license, an after-school job at a music store downtown, and a rusted Chevelle, and it wasn't odd for him to go out on any night of the week and not come home until some time the next day. I know my parents tried to confront him about his behavior, and I'm pretty sure they even tried seeing a counselor with him—they didn't necessarily hide the visits, but neither did they invite or inform me—but nothing really changed.

And then one Monday during Greg's senior year of

high school he left for school and didn't come back for four days.

Those were probably the four worst days of my life. My parents called the music store, but he hadn't shown up for his shift. They called his friends and his friends' parents, but none of them had seen him. They called everyone they could think to call, and then they called the police, but still: no Greg. People assured us they would keep their eyes peeled. Two police officers, an older man and a young woman, came to our house and asked a lot of questions, mostly of my parents, and mostly behind the closed folding doors of the family room while I waited upstairs. The only thing I heard was my mother raise her voice once, upset about something having to do with Greg's age, telling the officers, "Well I couldn't very well keep him from turning eighteen, could I? Unless you know how to make time stop, and if you do, please let me know." My father called me down a little while later, and in a very kind tone, with her head at a solicitous angle, the female officer asked, "Is there anything your brother ever told you that he asked you to keep secret? About people he knew, or places he went, or things he did? Did he share anything with you that might help us find him?" An acute wave of embarrassment washed over me—not because I had deep dark secrets to share about Greg, but because I *didn't* have any. Greg hadn't ever shared any secrets with me. I remember sitting silently in front of the police officers and feeling like a failure, like I wasn't really Greg's brother at all.

I went to school on those four days, and my parents went to work, and we came home and had dinner together. After dinner, I did my homework. We acted as if they were normal evenings. The silence in our house was massive and terrifying, broken only by my father stiffly climbing the stairs at the end of each evening to tell me he and my mother were going to bed, and that they loved me and hoped I knew that. I told him I did.

When I came home from school Friday afternoon, my brother was in his room, frantically shoving clothes from his dresser into black garbage bags. I almost didn't recognize him at first, because he'd cut his black hair down to short stubble that was dyed blonde, and he was wearing jeans and a white T-shirt. "Greg," I said stupidly. "You cut your hair."

"Thanks for letting me know," he said. "Now could you leave me alone?"

"Where have you been?"

"I don't have time right now, Sam. I'm out of here. For good."

"What do you mean? What about Mom and Dad?"

"What the fuck *about* Mom and Dad? Do you think they fucking care?"

"Yes."

"Here," he said, throwing a book toward me. I picked it up off the floor—it was an English version of *Towards a New Architecture*. "I'm replacing your book," he said. I turned to the title page, and there over the title was a stamp informing me that the book belonged to my father.

"This is Dad's," I said.

"It's the thought that counts," Greg said, still packing.

"Where are you going?"

"Don't worry. I'll be fine."

"But where are you going?"

"Sam!" he yelled loud enough that I flinched. Then, almost apologetically, he said, "I'm in kind of a hurry here.

Okay?" He didn't say anything more, and I stood there and watched him fill up his trash bags, and then followed him as he carried them downstairs and out the front door. I ran back up to his room and frantically looked for something I could grab that he couldn't leave without.

"Sam!" he called from downstairs. "Sam, I'm leaving." I didn't respond, because I was too focused on manically pulling random old games and notebooks and clothes out of Greg's closet, certain that I would find one perfect item that he couldn't do without. "Sam!" he called again, and then I heard the front door open and close. I kept pulling stuff out of his closet—torn magazines, faded concert t-shirts, stacks of weird fantasy role-playing cards, everything—and throwing it across his room. I wasn't even looking for anything specific anymore, really. I was just throwing his things, hard, against the band posters on the wall across the room, and I was crying, and repeating, "Fuck you, fuck you, fuck you!" over and over. And then I realized that I was tearing up my father's copy of *Towards a New Architecture*, but I couldn't stop myself, and I probably would have kept tearing it until it was only little shredded bits if I hadn't heard my father's voice somewhere outside the house.

When I ran out the front door and down the steps, my father was standing in the middle of our front lawn with his briefcase in his hand. Greg was on the sidewalk by his car, probably twenty feet away.

"So I guess that's just the way it goes," Greg was saying to my father.

"It doesn't have to be, Greg," my father said.

"But it's the way I want it to be, Dad!" my brother responded. "This is the fucking way I want it to be! You think something horrible's going to happen? It's not! I don't need this shit anymore!"

My father didn't say anything for a moment. When he did speak, what he said still, to this day, surprises me. He said, "You'll need to call your mother."

"I know," Greg said. Then he walked around the back of his car and opened the driver's door.

I looked at my father, watching him watch Greg. I felt that all my father had to do was say something—that he had the power to keep Greg from leaving, if only he would say the right words. But he didn't say anything at all. He just stood there, briefcase in hand, and watched as Greg climbed into his car, slammed the door, and started the engine. We both watched Greg drive down the street, and after his car disappeared around the corner, my father turned and walked right past me. Without saying a thing, he climbed our front steps, went into our house, and closed the door.

I sat on the front lawn for a long time. At first I stared at the point down the street where I'd last seen Greg's car. Then I stared at the spot along the curb where his car had been parked, the place on the sidewalk where he'd stood and told my father he was leaving. But finally I just stared at the lawn—the grass I was sitting on, the blades beneath my fingers—and I started pulling it out. I grabbed the grass tight in my fists and pulled, tossing the clumps away from me, where they fell in a little brown heap. I stopped only after I realized I'd completely destroyed a whole patch of grass, and the bare ground was showing through.

When I stood up and turned to go back inside the house, the color seemed off—our house was green, but in the winter light it looked gray. There seemed to be more steps up to the porch than I remembered, and I didn't remember the lattices as having been there before. The whole house seemed too far forward, as if it had slid toward the street. It looked structurally sound, but it didn't look like my house, and I realized that I couldn't picture the man that had just walked into it as being my father.

My mother drove up then. She waved to me as she pulled into the driveway. I couldn't remember her ever waving to me that way before. It was a forced, self-conscious wave, and both of us knew it. But there was a pleading in her expression, as if she were asking me to forgive her for the fraudulence of the gesture even as she made it. And I did. I waved right back. And I knew that after she parked the car in the garage and got out, she would go into the house, and I would follow her in. I had nowhere else to go. And although our house's floor plan must have been exactly the same as at least twenty other houses in the neighborhood, I knew our house was the only one I could walk through safely with my eyes closed if I wanted, because our house was the only one in which I knew where everything was.

Zero

"This time, I was stammering and saying nonsensical things when Mastroianni asked me about his part. He was so trusting. They all trusted me." –Fellini

He was in a cold gray ocean, swimming. Men and women young and old surrounded him, their expressions determinedly pleasant, but with a tightness to their smiles as they thrashed their arms and struggled, so close together, to stay afloat. When he rose on the crest of an immense, rolling wave, he saw that swimmers filled the water in every direction, as far as he could see, and on the white strip of distant shoreline even more swimmers were stepping from the sand into the surf. Then the wave passed and in its trough he saw only those nearest him—a woman with flawlessly applied eyeliner and red lipstick, wearing a bright white swimming cap, and an old man with short white hair, his face tan and creased. An odd current pushed them against one another, their limbs tangling. The woman and the old man panicked, grabbing at him from either side, clawing at his arms, his face, his head. He could see the whites of their frightened eyes as they pushed him under.

Beneath the surface, everyone's legs were pale and thrashing. Thigh muscles rippled beneath skin; a thousand feet paddled madly. He kicked further down, making his way to the ocean's flat, sandy floor, and when he looked up, the treading legs were just a soothing pulse far overhead, like blades of grass in the breeze. It was warm there on the ocean floor, and he lay down on the sand, relieved to have space. No sooner had he relaxed, though, than he felt an insistent, uncomfortable tug, and noticed a silvery thread extending upward from beneath the skin of his shoulder. Though he felt no pain, he watched in horror as the line grew taut and his flesh stretched, the curved outline of a hook plainly visible beneath his skin as he was pulled back toward the surface.

"Concocting another story of mysterious strangers?" a voice asked.

Charlie opened his eyes. "What?"

"We don't have to talk about it now," Alan said. "But you have to let me beat the shit out of you at some point." Alan pushed his glasses up his snub nose and gripped the steering wheel. He bared his teeth and polished them for a moment with the side of his index finger while the car's headlights carved a blue tunnel in the surrounding blackness. Fir trees flashed past the sides of the road, their ghostly trunks thin and pale.

"Where are we?" Charlie asked.

"We're almost there."

When they reached the small town, they drove slowly down the main street, looking for the hotel. The town's three stoplights glowed fuzzily in the damp night air, and the side streets extended only two or three blocks to the west before they vanished. The darkness beyond must be the ocean, Charlie thought. "What's it called?" he asked.

"Here it is," Alan said.

Hotel Anselmi, the sign read. Alan parked and they carried their bags into the lobby that was done up like an Arts and Crafts lodge, as if Frank Lloyd Wright had passed through recently, doling out Mission furniture and stained glass lampshades and the roaring fireplace beneath the long, walnut-stained mantel. On a flimsy plastic frame in the corner of the room was a placard welcoming them to the conference.

When the unshaven, sad-eyed desk clerk went into the back room to pull their receipts from the noisy computer printer, Alan turned to Charlie and smiled. "The dreams, for one, are ridiculous and obvious," he said. "They are amateurish and a cheat."

Charlie mimed embarrassment with an exaggerated shrug.

"I'm going to have to beat you at some point," Alan said. "And I'm going to beat you very, very badly. You'll probably be disfigured, but that's your own fault."

The clerk returned and handed them their silver room keys on cracked plastic rings.

"Real keys," Alan noted, examining his in his open palm as if it were an exotic insect. "Rustic—a nice touch. Are we too late for the dinner?"

The clerk assured them they were not, if they went in immediately.

"What about our bags?" Alan asked.

"Oh, they'll be taken care of," the clerk said.

Alan studied the man's face. "How many days since you've shaved?"

"Four," the man said, rubbing his chin. "I'm growing a beard."

"You are not," Alan said.

The dining room was through a door at the side of the lobby. Inside was a small bar tended by a small bartender with a crooked nose and large dark eyes with long lashes. Beyond the bar stood a dozen round tables dressed to impress in their formal beige tablecloths. Late diners still occupied a few of the tables, nursing glasses of wine or absently studying their empty plates. A black piano sat in the back corner, its polished surface gleaming. Along the back wall was a buffet with picked over entrées in heated silver trays of congealing sauces. "We've missed the better part of this," Charlie said.

"It's part of the package," Alan said, "which means we paid for it. Which means we eat."

They moved along the trays, filling their plates with what food remained.

"There's no controlling idea," Alan said. "It's completely fragmented. Is that chicken or potatoes? I would suggest that you need to be systematic, but I wonder: Can you be systematic if you don't have anything to say? The pasta looks okay. Because then: Systematic about what? I'm doing this in small doses because I want you to survive. Vegetables, yes, important. You'll be badly bruised, but you'll be stronger. The salad is wilted."

When they turned, a man at a table across the room beckoned them. It took Charlie a moment to realize that it was Lofton, his old boss from the ad agency. Lofton's hair had gone gray in the two years since Charlie had last seen him, and he'd added more pounds to his bearish frame, but he wore the hair and weight well. He was with a striking young woman with hazel eyes and long brown hair that lay upon an immaculate white sweater. Lofton smiled widely as he stood and shook Charlie's hand. "Ah, yes," Lofton said, pleased. "I wondered."

"What are you doing here?" Charlie asked as they all sat down together. "Following my career path?"

Lofton laughed. "To poverty and insecurity? No. I've been invited to speak about commercials. 'Techniques of Compressed Narrative,' they're calling it—we tell stories, too, you remember. This is Lisa."

The young woman acknowledged them with a nod and half-smile, and sipped her wine. Alan immediately began quizzing Lofton on what would be included in his presentation, but Charlie was distracted by the bartender, who beckoned to him. He excused himself from the table and crossed to the bar.

"There's a woman in the lobby says she'd like to have a word with you," the bartender said.

When he went out to the lobby, he found Sara sitting in an armchair by the fire, her back to him. Ivory sticks held her black hair up in a chignon, revealing her long, pale neck, and just when he was about to touch her shoulder, she turned. "Surprise!" she said.

"You didn't tell me," he said.

"Because it's a surprise," she said.

He felt warm and happy standing there in front of the fire as its soft light played on Sara's delicate face. "A wonderful surprise. You look beautiful."

"I do not," she said, touching her hair and smoothing her skirt. "I've been in a car. I'm staying at The Cove. It's not as nice as this place, but it's fine. I'm meeting some people for drinks—you should come."

"I've just sat down to dinner with Alan. My boss from my old job is in there, too."

She crinkled her face in distaste. "It's a room full of writer-types?"

"Mostly."

"Then I won't join you. Find me after."

"Where? Who are you meeting?"

"I think there's only one bar in town."

"May I kiss you?"

"No," she said, getting up. "Find me after." She headed toward the door, looked back once to smile, and then walked out into the night.

When Charlie returned to the dining room, Lofton was alone at their table. "Lisa will be right back," he said as if he'd been asked. "And your friend Alan said he didn't feel well."

"Alan rarely feels well."

"It's good to see you," Lofton said. "I was hoping to." He leaned toward Charlie as if preparing to divulge a great and humorous secret, but instead massaged Charlie's shoulder for a moment.

"Things are good at the agency?" Charlie asked.

"Of course. But you're wondering about Lisa, right?"

"You're married, aren't you?"

"No more. And you may congratulate me on that."

"Congratulations."

Lofton leaned back as if Charlie had insulted him. "You think I'm going through a mid-life crisis."

"I haven't seen you in two years," Charlie said. "I don't know what you're going through."

"She's an incredible girl. The best thing that's happened to me in years. I have more energy now than I've had since I can remember—since I was a kid. I could wrestle you to the ground right now."

"But could you pin me?"

"You think I'm in a crisis, but you wait. How old are you?"

"Forty-three."

"Still married?"

"Yes."

"You wait ten years, then you come talk to me." Lofton picked a loose thread from the shoulder of Charlie's shirt and tossed it aside. "We should get together. I miss you. The agency misses you. Remember the fun we used to have?"

Lisa returned and sat down, offering the same half-smile as before.

"I've told you about Charlie, haven't I?" Lofton said to her. "The campaigns we worked on together?"

"I don't know," she said.

"Incredible guy," Lofton said. "And a good man." He turned his attention back to Charlie. "So what are you working on?"

"A novel."

"See?" Lofton said, delighted. "Now he's a novelist."

"What's it about?" Lisa said.

"A robot."

The other two nodded gravely. "There's a good tradition of that," Lofton said.

The couple left after a bit, and Charlie became the last person in the dining room. The bartender beckoned again, and Charlie stood and walked to the bar. "Yes?" he said.

The bartender tipped his head toward the far end of the bar, and when Charlie turned, he was shocked to find his father seated on the last stool. "Dad!" he blurted.

The man wore his best suit, his hair was immaculately combed, and a glass of bourbon sat in front of him. He smiled and nodded, seeming tired, but pleased to be where he was.

"How is it that you're here?" Charlie said. "How are you?"

"I haven't heard from you," his father said.

"I'm well," Charlie said.

"You're successful?"

"I'm working hard."

"A happy family that you support?"

Charlie shrugged. "No children yet."

His father nodded as if he understood, but his disappointment was evident.

"I've never—" Charlie started. "I mean, I've wanted to talk to you about that."

"Of course," his father said. "There's always more to say."

"But about that," Charlie said. "About me."

"I've always loved you unconditionally," his father said. "Remember that."

"I know—I don't have a single complaint. But I worry. I want you to understand something. Or I feel like I want to describe something to you."

His father smiled and made as if he were going to pat Charlie's hand, but held off at the last instant, and raised his glass of bourbon instead.

"I don't know what I'm saying. I just wish we could talk more," Charlie said.

"There's always family and work and life," his father said. "People are busy."

"Yes."

His father patted the bar, lightly. "But I should go. I'm tired."

"We could have another drink," Charlie said.

His father smiled. "I'm not so young anymore," he said. "I'll see you again soon? Tomorrow?"

"I've always loved you unconditionally," his father said again as he stood. He thanked the bartender quietly and moved past Charlie, toward the lobby.

"Tomorrow," Charlie called to him, but his father just raised his hand in acknowledgment without turning around as he left the room. When Charlie turned back to the bartender, the man was busily drying glasses. "What do I owe you?" Charlie said.

"No charge," the man said.

After they'd finished and lay together in the dark for a few minutes, Charlie spoke. "Why do you do that?" he said. "Say you're meeting people when you're not?"

"I told you they didn't make it," Sara said, her voice small.

He pulled her close, her perfume sketching several lovely images for him. He buried his face in her hair, kissed the back of her neck. "Why do you do that, I ask you."

"Because I don't want you to think you have to entertain me."

They listened as a group of women, their hollow laughter echoing in the hallway, walked past their door. After the women were gone, they heard the muted hum of the ice machine at the end of the corridor. He kissed her again.

"You're going to lectures tomorrow that will make you better?" she said.

"Maybe."

"You'll have time to see me?"

"Yes."

"If you don't, you can tell me."

"I will," he said. "Have time to see you."

"You can tell me," she repeated drowsily.

He lightly kissed the back of her neck and they fell asleep, their bodies against one another.

They awoke to someone pounding on the door. The curtain was aglow with the morning sun.

"Wake up!" Alan called through the door. "It's time!"

Sara pulled the blanket over her head as Charlie put on his pants and a shirt and opened the door a few inches, bracing it with his foot. "I'm not quite ready," he said. "I'll be down in a few minutes."

"I'll come in and wait," Alan said. "You can absorb punishment while you get ready."

"I'm—the room's a mess," Charlie said. "I'll be down in a few."

"What's wrong?"

"I got drunk last night. The room's a mess. Let me meet you downstairs in a few minutes."

Alan studied him through the bit of open door. "Okay," he said suspiciously.

Charlie closed the door and turned back to the room.

Through the closed door Alan shouted, "I'm having fun!" His heavy steps headed away, down the hall.

Sara lowered the blanket from her head. "He scares me. Why do you hang around with him?"

"I don't know. He reads my stuff and gives me suggestions."

"You must be desperate for readers," she said.

Charlie looked around the empty room. "My bag," he said. "My bag isn't here."

He left the room and walked quickly down to the lobby, where a woman with frizzy red hair and thick red lipstick stood behind the front desk. When he asked about his bag, she checked under her counter and in the back room, and then picked up the phone and pushed a few worn buttons and consulted with whoever was at the other end of the line. No one knew anything about his bag. "Do you know the name of the person you left it with?" she asked.

"I didn't get his name," he said. "He was a young guy, growing a beard."

She wrinkled her forehead thoughtfully. "I can't think of any staff members that have a beard," she said.

"*Growing* a beard," he said.

"Well, I'll definitely keep looking for it, sir," she said. "I'll check with housekeeping and I'll check with hospitality. I'll make some inquiries."

When he turned away from the desk, he noticed his sister sitting in the corner of the high-backed sofa in front of the lobby fireplace. Bouncing a doll on her knee, she couldn't have been older than seven or eight, and as he stepped around the front of the sofa he found a smaller boy sitting dutifully next to her. The boy was dressed in corduroy pants and an ill-fitting sweater and held a stuffed monkey in his lap while he watched his big sister comb her doll's honey-colored hair. When a woman moved past him toward the children, he knew immediately that it was his mother. "Let's go, your father's waiting," she said.

His sister jumped to her feet and picked up a small backpack from the floor. The boy slid carefully off the sofa and then turned back to grab his stuffed animal.

"Where is your bag?" his mother asked the boy.

The boy looked down at his feet and then back at his mother as if she might answer her own question.

"What did you do with your bag?" she asked. "Stephanie, where is your brother's bag?"

"I don't know," his sister said.

"Wonderful. This is just what we need. Young man, *where is your bag?*"

"I had it," the boy said, nervously rubbing one hand with the other. "I don't know."

"For Christ's sake," his mother said. "I'll go back and check the room. Stay *right here*." As she walked away from the boy and toward Charlie, she shook her head in an expression of adult solidarity. "His mind just *wanders*," she said as she passed him on her way out of the lobby.

"What did you do with it?" his sister asked the boy.

"I don't know," the boy said. The fire in the fireplace crackled encouragement.

"You have to keep track of your stuff," she said.

"I *know*," he said.

"You're holding us up," Alan said, suddenly at Charlie's side, grabbing him by the arm. "I've already eaten. I'll sit with you, though, so we can get started."

"They've lost my bag," Charlie said.

"My bag was in my room," Alan said. "Did you check your room?"

"It wasn't there. My manuscript was in that bag. I had notes and things written all through it."

"It's okay, I have my copy," Alan said. "I'm ready to kick your ass."

As Alan pulled him toward the dining room, Charlie turned back to see his mother leading the two children out the lobby's front door. His sister had her doll and bag, but the little boy had nothing. At the last second, the boy darted back and grabbed the stuffed monkey from where it lay by a leg of the sofa, and then ran to catch up with the others.

"Overloaded with forced, generic sentimentality," Alan said, waving Charlie's manuscript in the air as Charlie ate his eggs and toast. "Actually, I can't even say if it's sentimentality. Sentimentality is bad enough, but this is almost just a gesture at sentimentality, or at nostalgia, or at something, but a something that's not there. And thank god it's not there, because I can't stand sentimentality or nostalgia. They reek of death and lies. And the meaning is completely obscure. Or it's so fragmentary that it's meaningless, like the stringing together of leftovers, or a rack of factory irregulars. This is okay that I'm doing this, right?"

Charlie nodded.

"We understand the robot is talking to the therapist. But then to suggest that the robot had a childhood raises any number of real-world questions. How, we wonder? Was he physically smaller? Or just stupider? It seems that he had the childhood only so you could put his memories of it in the book, right? There's no reason for it except to intrude on what I would normally call the main story, but here I'm not sure there is one. The story is like a man who keeps walking into the same empty room, saying, 'Excuse me,' and then leaving. Wait—it's like a robot that does that, which is even more annoying."

Charlie ate his eggs. He buttered a piece of toast and spread jelly across it and took a bite.

"I know these fragments might mean something to you," Alan said, "but not everything that interests you will interest other people. The reader has to understand why he's reading."

"I understand," Charlie said. "I understand what you're saying, I mean."

"I haven't even gotten specific yet," Alan said. "I'm not even drawing blood. Here." He pushed a pamphlet across the table to Charlie. *The Anselmi Beach Writing Workshops*, its cover read in fancy print, below which it trumpeted, in bold lettering:

ASA FLAHERTY REVEALS
"THE ELEMENTS OF NARRATIVE"

DENISE LANISI LEADS YOU TO YOUR
"AUTHENTIC VOICE/AUTHENTIC SELF"

ALBERTO MASA "MASSAGES THE SCENE"

Charlie flipped quickly through the pamphlet. Lofton's name was in small print on the last page, under the heading "Other Sessions."

"Will they be signing their books, do you think?" Alan asked. "I brought Flaherty and Masa's books."

"I didn't know you'd read their stuff."

"I didn't finish either of them, but still. You're wearing the same clothes you had on yesterday."

"I told you they lost my bag."

"You're lucky you overdress for everything."

On their way out, Charlie stopped at the front desk to ask about his bag. Instead, the clerk told him she'd just received a phone call for him. Confused, he pulled his cell phone from his pocket to make sure it was working. "Cell phone service is pretty spotty here," she said. "You can retrieve the message on the lobby phone if you want."

"But my bag," he said.

"I'm looking for it," she said. "Intently. I assure you, sir."

The message was from his wife. He called her back, and when she asked how things were going, he unthinkingly said, "It's great here—you should come out." He listened to his own words in a state of dismay, baffled as to why he had said them and immediately searching for a way to try and reinterpret what he had said, so that he hadn't actually said it.

"Now?" she said. "But I thought you needed to get away—some time alone. Are you still having the headaches?"

"On and off. Less, though."

"And you're not trying to get any work done, right? You're just going to the talks."

"I know," he said. "I'm trying to relax and concentrate. To focus."

"Are you serious about me coming out there, or are you just being nice? What about Alan?"

"Alan can take care of himself. We could go to dinner," Charlie said, feeling the exchange had moved out ahead of his thoughts and he could not now catch up. "You could shop while I go to the last workshops tomorrow morning, I guess."

"We said this would be a weekend for you to relax alone. And the doctor said to see if relaxing helps with the headaches."

"I'm sure I can still relax with you here," he said, annoyed now with both her and himself.

"Okay," she said. "If you say it's okay."

"I'm telling you it's okay."

"Okay," she repeated.

The workshops were held in the Anselmi Beach Community Center, a modest one-story wood building on a rocky bluff that overlooked the ocean. The crashing waves below sent up a constant spray that beaded and streaked the windows on the ocean side of the main conference room, where thirty or forty people sat in short rows of plastic chairs. The first workshop was led by Asa Flaherty, a man well over six feet tall and built like a football lineman. Dark chest hair sprouted from under the neck of his red polo shirt and he leaned on the podium in a way that seemed to threaten the structure's safety. Flaherty said a little about the importance of characters, and then the importance of recognizable goals, and then some things about clarity of conflict. After about twenty minutes, Charlie stood up.

"How much are you being paid to tell us the obvious?" he asked.

Asa regarded him drowsily. "How much did you pay to hear it?"

"How can you look yourself in the mirror when you realize you've cheapened your talent by peddling a false version of it in the literary equivalent of a pyramid scheme?" Charlie said.

"There are four kinds of creative people," Asa said. "Some like the idea of creating, but really prefer just to talk about it. Some actually create, and hate talking about it." The podium finally gave way, splintering beneath Flaherty. Pieces of broken wood tumbled across the carpet as the crowd gasped. Flaherty picked up a long piece that had been part of the side and, as he made his way toward Charlie, wielded it like a club. "Some people like both things, to create and to talk about creating. And some like neither. Which are you?"

Charlie scrambled over the others in his row, trying to

escape to the opposite aisle before Flaherty reached him. "That last category is the absence of creativity," Charlie said as he struggled to get through, "so you really only have three kinds of creative people, not four."

"That's the first correct thought you've had in years," Flaherty growled, pushing the others in Charlie's row out of the way. When he got within range, he raised the piece of wood high over his head and brought it down with all his might on Charlie's back.

"This guy's good," Alan whispered, nudging Charlie with his elbow. "Look at how he handles the microphone. He's like a rock star—like Jim Morrison."

Charlie watched Flaherty pause for a moment to consult his notes. "I'd like to move on now to the importance of climax," Flaherty murmured into the microphone. The sound of the workshop participants turning their notebooks to a fresh page was momentarily deafening.

Sara didn't show up at the coffee shop they'd agreed on for lunch. When Charlie got through to her room at her hotel, she answered weakly. "I'm not well," she said.

"What's wrong?"

"Something I ate."

"I'll be right there. Can I bring you anything?"

"Don't come," she said. "I'll be fine."

"Don't be ridiculous," he said.

When he got to her room, he found her in bed, sweating through cotton pajamas and shivering beneath the blankets.

"I told you not to come," she said. "I don't want you to see me like this."

"I wanted to make sure you're alright."

"I'm fine," she said, closing her eyes. "But I'm glad you came. Secretly."

He brushed a lock of damp hair from her face and placed his hand against her forehead. "We should call a doctor."

"I'll be fine," she said. "Do you remember when we met? At the resort?"

"Yes." A tension built in his head. He felt as if his eyelids had suddenly grown swollen and slack.

"I was with Gary," she said. "Remember, he skipped all the meetings to golf? I got sick then, too."

"I didn't know that," he said. He thought about skipping the afternoon workshops. He could walk up into the hills on the other side of the highway and look down at the town and the ocean, he thought. And then maybe he could find some soft pine needles to lie down on and sleep.

Denise LaNisi was rail thin, wore loose vintage clothes, had long gray hair and thick glasses, and spoke so earnestly into the microphone that her *S*'s came out of the speakers as pure sibilant distortion. She challenged the writers in the workshop to stop censoring themselves. She challenged them to write only truth. She challenged them to write that truth from the site of their most authentic self.

Charlie interrupted her. "Isn't this just new age claptrap with a literary veneer?" he called out. "Writing as a warm fuzzy self-help experience?"

"I'm not sure who said that," Denise said, peering into the audience. "But don't you write because you want to understand something about your most authentic, autonomous self?"

"Isn't the idea of a single, authentic self false?" Charlie said. "What if we don't believe in the self?"

"Has your lack of belief in the self led you to freedom and happiness?" she asked.

"Maybe freedom isn't happiness," he said.

"So is that why you're writing about a robot?" she said. "Because you don't believe in the human self? Or is it because you aren't ready to recognize it?"

"Yeah," Alan said next to him, nodding. "Which is it, Charlie?"

"Is that why you're unable to create a convincing love relationship?" Denise continued. "Because you don't know how to love? Because you don't even believe you have a self that exists to love or to be loved? And so you substitute sex for love and robots for people? This is the artistic statement you've thrown your career away to make? Destruction as expression?"

The rest of the workshop participants turned toward him, nodding in agreement. "You're a joke," a woman a few rows away hissed.

Charlie stood to leave.

"Where are you going?" Alan whispered. "This is inspiring."

"I've got a headache," he said. "I'm going outside for a minute."

"I'll take notes," Alan said.

Charlie slipped out of the room while Denise enumerated the ways in which writers censored themselves. Many of the workshop participants nodded in agreement.

The cool ocean breeze felt good on his face as he walked down a long set of wooden steps to the beach. He slipped his shoes off, pushed his socks inside them, and stepped onto the beach, feeling the sand between his toes. He hadn't walked far before he came upon Lofton's girlfriend sitting on the beach, reading a book. He said hello, and she smiled at him. "Where's Lofton?" he asked.

She pointed toward the ocean, and there in the surf was Lofton. He wore chaotically colored swimming trunks, and his chest hair was plastered to his skin in wet swirls. He came out of the water and walked up the sand, beaming like the happiest man on the planet.

"Put your suit on and join me," he said. "Lisa has to read."

"It's only seventy degrees out. Isn't the water freezing?" Charlie said.

"It's perfect!" Lofton boomed. "It's invigorating! Watch." He ran down the beach and into the water again, dove into the surf, and then came to the surface and waved to them. "Both of you! Join me!" he yelled, and then swam out further, away from the beach.

Charlie sat down in the sand next to Lisa. "What are you reading?"

"Wittgenstein," she said. "I'm in a master's program in philosophy."

"You're a student," he said, surprised.

"You mean young," she said. "Too young to be with your friend."

"Women as young and beautiful as yourself aren't often seen with someone like Lofton."

She laughed. "He's creative and fun. He lives with enthusiasm. He engages life."

Charlie nodded. "Maybe that's what I'm looking for. Enthusiasm."

"You have enthusiasm for your writing, don't you? Or you wouldn't be here."

"Maybe I came here to try and find it."

"I see. Has it worked?"

He looked out to the water, where Lofton was performing a relaxed backstroke far from the shore. "I quit working for Lofton at the agency because I thought I had something important to say, something more important than anything else in my life. Something that was unique and had to be said and had nothing to do with a website or a campaign or creating a brand, something completely apart from what I was doing. The more I work on it, though, the more confused I get about what that thing might be. I wonder if maybe I don't really have anything to say, after all."

Lisa laughed again.

"Why do you laugh?" he asked.

"Because you're a funny person. So serious."

He smiled. "You should read my novel if you want to laugh."

"I will, if you give it to me."

"There you are," a voice said in mock outrage. They turned to see Alan standing over them, hands on hips. "You missed a great workshop. I'm going to write nothing but truth from now on. That's what it's all about."

Charlie's wife, Anne, tossed aside a glossy fashion magazine she'd been looking at when he walked to where she was sitting in front of the fireplace in the hotel lobby. With her fashionable glasses, short haircut, and athletic build, she looked like a tennis player between tournaments. She offered him her cheek, which he dutifully kissed. "Have you been waiting long?" he asked.

"You're wearing the same clothes you had on yesterday."

"They've lost my bag." He rubbed the bridge of his nose as if it were related to the bag's disappearance.

"And we can't afford for you to buy some new clothes?"

"I haven't had time. I've been going to the meetings."

"Where did you have it last?"

"I didn't lose it," he said irritably. "They took my bag when I got here. Then it disappeared."

"You just left it with someone?"

"Can we not discuss this right now? Could we just not worry about it?"

She shrugged. "Where are we going to dinner?"

They went to an Italian restaurant run by a German couple that had moved to the coast after closing a successful French restaurant they'd run in Chicago for two decades. The dinner was part of the workshop program for the weekend, and most of the faces that had filled the conference room in the community center were there. But Charlie and Anne hadn't even finished their salads when Anne's face tightened. She set her fork down.

"Your friend is here," she said, looking across the room.

"Who?" Charlie asked. "Alan?"

"With Alan."

He turned. Alan sat at a table for two, and across from him, her back to them, was Sara. When she turned her head to the side he could see her smiling as if Alan was greatly entertaining.

"Sara," he said.

"I know her name," Anne said.

"We ran into her earlier."

"Don't. I don't want to hear your story."

"It's a coincidence."

"A fantastic coincidence," she said. "The odds are staggering. Is she a writer now?"

"Yes. Or wants to be."

"Is *that* what she wants?"

"Please don't start."

"I don't think I'm the one who started it," she said.

They finished their salads in silence. When the teenaged waitress took their plates away, Anne put her napkin on the table and reached down to get her purse from the floor.

"What's wrong?" he asked.

"Do you seriously think I can sit here and have dinner with you while I'm looking at her across the room?" Anne said. "Who do you think you are?"

"I told you it's a coincidence," he said. "I'm sorry, I don't have control over who decides they want to become a writer. I wish I did, but I don't. These workshops are popular."

Anne shook her head as if trying to clear it of some confusion. "No," she said. "That's not right. I'm not doing this. This whole thing is a joke. This meal, that slut, your whole decision that you're now a fucking *artiste*, this whole marriage: it's all just a tired joke. This is not the life we've built. You can eat by yourself." She stood and walked out of the restaurant without looking back. He didn't go after her.

Later, after Charlie had finished his lasagna in silence, Alan came over. "Your wife wasn't feeling well?" he asked.

"No. What happened to Sara?"

"She said she had to go meet some people, but that I should tell you she's sorry she wasn't able to say hello. Would now be a good time for me to give you my full critique? The real body blows that will soften you up for the knockout?"

"No."

"Ah," Alan said, as if sensing for the first time that something wasn't right. "Then later. I'll surprise you in the dark, like a mugger."

There was a sudden crash from across the room, and Asa Flaherty stood up from a dining table that had shattered beneath the weight of his massive forearms. He walked angrily toward Charlie's table, but Charlie, catching Flaherty's eye, tipped his head discreetly toward Alan. Flaherty shifted his focus, and it took the man just a few immense strides to reach their table, pick Alan up by the back of his shirt, and throw him to the floor in the middle of the room. Several diners jumped up and joined Flaherty as he mercilessly pummeled Alan. Charlie applauded.

"What about early tomorrow morning?" Alan asked, still standing next to Charlie's table. "Before the official schedule starts, so you have the day to recover?"

Charlie massaged his temples. "I don't know. I don't know."

"Okay," Alan said. "But I want to get it done this weekend. I'm in perfect shape, the material is fresh in my mind, and my stamina is tremendous. We could go rounds and rounds and I'd never tire of delivering the punishment. Here's a sampler: did you notice how many scenes you end with the robot's analyst saying something pithy? It's a crutch."

"Alan," Charlie pleaded.

"Okay," Alan said, backing away. "We'll talk later." He turned and walked out the same door Anne had. Like her, he didn't look back.

Sara was standing barefoot on the sand in the dark, her back to the water, the breeze twisting her skirt around her legs. Charlie stood up the beach from her with his hands in his pockets. Behind her he could see the moon low in the sky, its reflection broken across the water's dark surface. "She just left, without saying anything else?" Sara asked.

"She just left," he said.

"Are you angry?"

"Yes."

"At me?"

"Yes."

"Why?"

"Why did you come to the restaurant with Alan?"

"He saw me in the lobby and recognized me as your friend. He invited me."

"Why were you in the lobby of my hotel?"

"I was looking for you. You didn't tell me your wife was coming. I only found out she was here when Alan invited me to dinner. I had to pretend to ask Alan if you were here, too, as if I didn't know. He said yes, that you'd be at the restaurant with your wife."

"So you came to the restaurant to watch us."

"I told you, Alan invited me. You want me to eat dinner alone in my room? I already spent the whole day in my room. I was sick, remember?"

"I didn't say I wanted you to stay in your room."

Sara turned and moved toward the surf, to where the expiring waves splashed up onto her ankles. The water shimmered in the moon's weak light. "This feels good," she said, stepping toward the waves. "You should take off your shoes and try it."

"I'm sure it's ice cold," he said.

Sara turned to him as a wave splashed around her shins. "Don't you want to fuck me tonight?" she said. "Charlie?"

He watched her move further toward the waves. "It's too cold to be in the water," he said. "Come back."

"You didn't answer my question."

"I don't want to answer any questions."

She continued into the surf. A wave came in knee high, and she wobbled uncertainly as it pushed past her.

"You still want to fuck me?" she called up the beach to him.

"You're making me nervous. Come back up here."

"Come into the water. It feels good."

"These are my only clothes," he said.

A wave hit her mid-thigh, knocking her off balance. She put a hand down through the water to brace herself, but the suction of the receding water pulled her off her feet. She let out a loud, girlish giggle as the water pulled her further away until she found her balance again and stood up, soaked. "Charlie," she called, but the next wave hit her in the back, knocking her off her feet as its silver crest moved over her.

He could see her rolling in the surf and heard her coughing as he sprinted across the wet sand and into the water. When he took her arm, she was coughing more and also laughing, and he was surprised at how cold she was already, and how thin her arm felt in his grip—he was afraid he was bruising her as he grabbed her above the elbow and pulled her out of the waves. When they were safely back on the beach, she turned and kissed him roughly. Taking her by the hand, he led her up the beach and toward the street that led to the hotel.

After Sara took a hot shower and fell asleep on the bed, he took a shower, too, and then wrung his black wool pants out as well as he could and put them back on, along with the same gray dress shirt he'd been wearing. When he went down to the bar, the same bartender was there, waiting.

"Do you really get enough business to keep regular hours like this?" Charlie asked as the man poured some whiskey.

"We only stay open late when the writers are in town."

"That's a stereotype, you know."

"And yet here we are," the man said, placing the drink on the bar in front of Charlie.

It was then that he noticed his sister a few stools down. Her hair was exactly as it had been before it fell out, light brown with some faint strands of gray. She was smoking a cigarette and watching him.

"Emily," he said. "I saw you with Mom this morning. I hoped I'd get a chance to talk to you."

"Did you ever find your bag?" she asked.

He laughed as he extended an arm and leg to reveal the state of his clothing. "Would I look like this if I had?"

She brought her drink and cigarette with her as she moved down to take the stool next to him. "You were never very good at keeping track of your things," she said.

"No," he agreed, examining her face.

"Surprised?" she said.

"You were too young."

"I used to think that, but not anymore. I had my time. There aren't any guarantees."

"Still smoking, though."

She laughed as she held the cigarette up for inspection. "What does it matter now?" she said.

Anne walked into the room, with Sara at her side. They were smiling.

"The two of you together," Charlie said as they took seats at one of the tables. "Now, that's better."

"You didn't think we were going to leave you alone

tonight?" Anne said, and Sara laughed as if Anne had made a clever little joke.

And then Ellen, the woman he'd dated before he met his wife, came into the room. She was tall and thin, and though she, too, smiled, it was with the sardonic quality that he remembered about her. She kissed him on the cheek and took a seat at another table.

"What a pleasant coincidence," he said.

And then Carrie came in. He had lived with her before he met Ellen. She, too, kissed him on the cheek, and took a seat at a table.

"Will it be all of you, then?" he asked.

"Of course," Carrie said. "There's nothing we wouldn't do for you."

His sister stubbed out her cigarette and stood. "This is my cue to leave."

"But we've barely talked," he said.

She nodded toward the door—another woman was stepping into the room. "You seem a bit busy right now," she said. She smiled, patted him lightly on top of his head, and headed toward the door.

One by one, the women he'd known came into the bar, kissed him on the cheek, and found places to sit at the tables. The last was the girl he'd gone to his high school prom with, though she was a woman now, his own age. "Jenny," he said, surprised. "You look great. But nothing happened between us, did it?"

"I'm married," she said, kissing him on the cheek and ignoring his question. "I have three children, all girls."

When Jenny found a seat at the bar, Anne raised her glass. "A toast," she called out, and all of the women raised their glasses. "To Charlie! We're better for having known you, we're grateful to have loved you."

"To have been loved by you!" one of them said as if it were a correction. Charlie couldn't tell who'd said it, but everyone laughed. Proud and embarrassed, he raised his glass, and everyone drank. The bartender poured glasses of champagne and distributed them to the women, and there was more laughter and talk among them.

Then Lofton's girlfriend Lisa stepped into the room. She walked up to the bar and, after politely saying hello to Charlie, asked the bartender for Scotch.

"You drink Scotch?" Charlie said.

"It's for Lofton," she said. "He's not feeling well."

"I meant to go to his talk."

She shook her head. "It didn't turn out like he expected. He got some questions he didn't count on."

Some of the women brought their empty glasses to the bar and headed toward the door, but Charlie remained focused on Lisa. "You don't want a drink?" he asked. "I'll buy you one if you'd like."

She raised an eyebrow with undisguised suspicion. "What happened to your friend?"

"Which one?" he asked. All of the other women had returned their glasses and made their exit by then, except for Sara and his wife, though they, too, were headed toward the door. When they waved to him, he nodded quickly in their direction, and they went out the door arm in arm, laughing.

"The one who was with you last night," Lisa said.

"She's at her own hotel," he said.

Lisa laughed. "It was a man. He sat down to dinner with us."

"Oh," Charlie said, flustered. "That was Alan. I don't know where he is."

The bartender placed the Scotch in front of Lisa.

"Did you want one for yourself?" Charlie asked again. "On me."

"You're cute," she said, as if he were a stumbling toddler. She picked up Lofton's drink and left the room.

The bartender offered Charlie a sympathetic look. "I think she does like you," he said.

"I amuse her. That's not necessarily liking."

The bartender shrugged. "She's with someone else."

Charlie looked around the empty room. The tables were clean and straight. There was no sign anyone had been there. He felt a sense of emptiness settle over him. "I'm not sure I belong here," he said.

"Of course not," the bartender said. "You don't belong anywhere."

"But I mean I might be doing the wrong kind of work."

"If you stopped, though."

Charlie tried to picture it, but no images or feelings came to him. "I think I would disappear."

"There would be no reason for you," the bartender said. "So you should probably keep doing it, if only for your health."

As he tried to meet the man's gaze, Charlie felt the aura of what he knew would be another headache, and he closed his eyes. "Did someone get the drinks?" he asked.

"No. I'll charge them to your room."

Charlie thanked the man and walked back up to his room. When he got there, though, Sara was gone. The only evidence that she had been there were the rumpled bedclothes. They smelled of saltwater.

"There are too many characters," Alan said at breakfast the next morning. "Are you going to take notes?"

"I'm listening," Charlie said. "I'll remember."

"Well, I've written it all in the margins," Alan said doubtfully, "so I suppose that's okay. But listen, I think the difficulty stems from the very concept of the thing. The fundamental problem is just your basic idea."

Charlie nodded.

"You give the robot interiority and a creative faculty. He can see things other people can't."

"Memories."

"But no," Alan said. "That's bad enough, a robot with memories. But no, some of them are fantasies. You have a robot with memories and a robot with fantasies. You're either a genius or an idiot. So has the MacArthur Foundation contacted you recently? That's what we need to know."

"Tell me this, Alan," Charlie said. "What are *you* working on?"

"Something."

"I've never seen it."

"It's not ready."

"When will it be?"

"Who can say?" Alan said, dismissing the question with a shrug. "But you're derailing the discussion. This always happens when the author is allowed to speak. Maybe we should proceed under workshop rules. You can't say anything."

"Okay."

"No more."

"I agreed."

"Stop."

Charlie made a show of silence. He drank his orange juice and drummed his fingers.

"Okay," Alan said, "I've made a list of your bad habits. Telling instead of showing. Disorienting the reader by starting scenes with dialogue. Implying any number of relationships without ever clearly defining them for the reader. Complete lack of background or exposition. Goalless characters. Writing without any meaning or message. Wallowing in a shallow nostalgia or sentimentality. Writing without any sense of where you're headed, which is really just another way of saying: no structure. An alarmingly sexist attitude toward women—and you should know that as an enlightened person, I am outright offended by it. An inability to portray even one character as sympathetic…"

When Charlie noticed Lisa peering into the room from the doorway, he continued nodding as if he were still listening. He assumed Lisa was looking for Lofton, but when her gaze met his, she pointed at him and motioned for him to come to her. "Excuse me for a minute," he said.

"No, the writer doesn't speak," Alan said. He continued listing Charlie's weaknesses, even as Charlie stood and crossed the room.

"Take a walk with me," Lisa said when he reached the doorway.

He looked back at Alan, who, frowning at Charlie's manuscript, carefully drew an X over an entire page.

"Okay," Charlie said.

Out on the street, the morning breeze was cool. Lisa walked quickly along the sidewalk, and Charlie matched her pace. She said nothing.

"It's a nice morning," he said eventually.

Lisa just nodded. When they got to the end of the street, she took the stairs down to the beach eagerly, hopping gracefully onto the sand without a sound. She slipped her shoes off and set them next to the stone beach wall, and Charlie did the same.

"A walk along the beach," he said. "It's a good idea."

She smiled as they walked toward the water. "You did the right thing," she said.

"What do you mean?"

"Losing your bag."

"I didn't lose it intentionally."

She laughed again, the same laugh that had punctuated each of their conversations. "Of course not."

"Do you not believe me?"

"No." They were near the water, and she slipped off her shorts and top and tossed them to the sand, revealing a white one-piece swimsuit she wore beneath. The whiteness of the suit stood in stark contrast to her tan, lightly freckled arms and legs.

"Have you ever thought of being an actress?" he said.

"No."

"I don't understand what we're doing."

She put her finger to her lips. "Sometimes silence is best," she said. She walked confidently into the water and then turned around and motioned for him to join her.

"But these are my only clothes. What if someone steals them?" he said.

"Why would someone steal them?" she said. "They're ruined."

He smiled, and felt a sense of relief as he removed the clothes. He walked down the beach in his boxer shorts, and stepped through the slowly breaking waves until he was able to lower himself into the water. He followed Lisa as she swam smoothly and confidently through the surf. When they had made their way beyond the breaking waves, he looked nervously back toward the beach before turning to see her still ahead of him. "How far are we going to go?"

he called to her. She treaded water for a moment so that she could look back at him, but then continued swimming without responding, moving further out.

She was stronger than him. As they continued away from the shore, there were times that the crest of a wave rose between them, and she would disappear. He did his best to keep up—though he knew he would get tired soon, too tired to hold any hope of making it back to shore—and when the next wave caught and raised him, he would see her again, just ahead, a figure in the water. So he kept on. He made his way through the cold gray ocean, swimming.

PETERSON WINS PRITZKER

The Mall of the Rockies, designed by American architect Nathan Peterson, just before the mall's completion in 1995. Peterson won the Pritzker Prize, architecture's most prestigious award, on Saturday. (AP photo)

LUCERNE, Switzerland (AP) – Nathan Peterson, whose challenging architectural style marks locations from Florida to Oregon and Iceland to Rio de Janeiro, has been named winner of the Pritzker Prize, architecture's most prestigious award. Peterson, 52, was informed of the award Saturday, and becomes the ninth American architect to win in the contest's thirty year history.

Many in the international architecture community were surprised by the award, as Peterson's ideas, often highly theoretical, have not often translated into the high profile projects that mark the work of previous Pritzker winners. His refusal to compromise his theoretical beliefs or temper idiosyncratic personal interests, combined with a career that has had its share of scandal, has estranged him from many of his peers and earned him a reputation as a confrontational designer working alone in the architectural avant-garde.

"I thought he was still in an institution. Was he not institutionalized?" Frank Gehry said upon being notified of Peterson's award.

Renzo Piano expressed concern for the Pritzker's integrity. "The award is not intended to be given to those who engage in professional versions of adolescent vandalism," Piano said.

Responding from Lucerne, where he maintains a residence, Peterson said, "I don't give a fig for the Pritzker. This is just an attempt to co-opt me into the mainstream, media-ready world of the ridiculous 'starchitects,' whom I embarrass on a regular basis.

"Two of the people on the jury this year have, at different times in the past, actually spit on me. One of them, and he knows who he is, was stupid enough to start a fistfight with me, which he lost in grand and embarrassing fashion. I'm not going to be tricked into creating some public persona so I can get profiled in *The New Yorker*."

Many see the award as justification for the many years Peterson, an outspoken critic of former Pritzker winners including Gehry, Piano, Rem Koolhaas, and Zaha Hadid, has spent actively fighting the contemporary style and demands of mainstream architecture. The jury cited Peterson's "ability to challenge assumptions of beauty, to deconstruct notions of form and function, and to pursue an uncompromising commitment to artistic statement.

"Through relentless analysis, confrontation, and sheer energy, Peterson has forged a body of work that has only grown more impressive with time. His designs, which invert expectations through their value of space over matter, penetrate to the core of our principles regarding how humans organize their structures and environments," the jury wrote.

Peterson alluded to his popular reputation as a "deconstructive" architect in his statement. "I'm not deconstructive," he said. "I'm destructive. There's a huge difference between those two things, and it mainly has to do with caring. Caring is something I've never been able to do, and I doubt I'll start anytime soon."

As a child in rural Montana, Peterson was held accountable for the burning down of storage sheds on three different ranches. None of the owners pressed charges, but when one of them demanded a written apology, the nine-year-old Peterson sent the man a two-word note: "You're welcome."

The Pritzker comes with a $100,000 grant, which will be awarded to Peterson on May 30. "I'll accept the thing so I can wear the ridiculous medallion to a discotheque, and I intend to blow the money on liquor and whores," he said. It's unclear what kind of ceremony the jury will organize should Peterson fail to attend.

"Wasn't he convicted of sex crimes?" Hadid asked upon hearing of Peterson's selection. "The man's a criminal, yes?"

Fired from an early teaching job at the University of

Wisconsin over charges of sexual harassment, Peterson has alternated between completely ignoring and commenting candidly on the controversies, often lurid, that have dogged his career. At the time of the Wisconsin firing, Peterson was quoted as saying, "There were at least three girls there at the time, so how is it possible that two of them were having a good time and only one felt harassed? Shouldn't the majority rule? I would have unlocked the door if [the accuser] really wanted to put her clothes on and leave, but she didn't use the safe word."

Peterson established Lothario, his design firm, the next year. The University of Wisconsin alerted authorities when more than a dozen graduate and undergraduate architecture students dropped out in order to accept employment at Lothario, but no wrongdoing was found. Peterson won his first award four years later, for a highway rest stop composed entirely of intersecting tinted glass panels. The rest stop was destroyed by vandals only three years later, but for the next two decades, Peterson continued to work primarily on local businesses and small public buildings, often lavishing his greatest attentions on restrooms.

He gained regional notoriety in the early 1980s when, in a contentious divorce trial, Peterson's wife Natalie described their sex life in great detail.

"We hadn't yet been married a year when Nathan told me he trusted me so much that he was willing to have anal sex with me," Natalie Peterson stated in a trial during which she accused the architect of emotional and physical abuse. "I refused, which he claimed was a sign of mistrust. We argued about it. Eventually, under extreme and constant verbal pressure from Nathan, I consented."

Peterson was quoted as having shouted at that moment

in the trial, "But ask her if she liked it!" at which point he was removed from the courtroom. Peterson has since refused comment on the divorce.

As a teen, Peterson attacked and seriously beat his maternal uncle at a family barbecue. Shocked, the family asked for an explanation. "I just wanted to see if I could do it. He's a grown man, so if he let me beat him, it seems to me it's his own fault," Peterson said. He then demanded a Dr. Pepper and some time alone "to put this event in perspective."

It wasn't until the early 1990s that Peterson developed a national profile, again through controversy, when without informing the city of Wischnatau, Wisconsin, he placed only a glass wall between the men's and women's showers in the locker rooms of a largely-glass building he designed for Wischnatau's largest outdoor swimming pool. Through the use of vents and a specialized glass coating Peterson's firm developed especially for the project, the glass wall's surface was designed to become opaque with condensed steam as soon as a shower spigot was turned on in either shower room. Pool users complained that the wall remained translucent in the interval between entering the room and starting the shower, and that nothing prevented other patrons from simply wiping the steam from the glass with their hands, thereby obtaining a clear view of the adjacent showers.

Peterson refused to alter the structure, claiming he had fulfilled his contractual obligation to create separate men's and women's locker rooms, and pointed out that blueprints for the building had at all times carried an abbreviated notation indicating the wall would be composed of glass. "The building is about vulnerability, the human body, and temptation," Peterson said at the time. The city of Wischnatau claimed Peterson deliberately confused and misled local officials, and a resulting lawsuit was further complicated when Peterson was arrested and charged with indecent exposure in a public restroom while in town to attend a court proceeding.

The Wischnatau, Wisc. City Pool House, designed by American architect Nathan Peterson, led to controversy early in his career. (AP photo)

"Apparently, men in Wischnatau can't touch other men in Wischnatau," Peterson told a local reporter. "And if you're wondering why the men of Wischnatau want to touch each other, look at the women."

The locker room lawsuit ended in a settlement that crippled Lothario's finances. The city hired a local contractor to cover the glass wall with traditional tiling, and Peterson's website officially lists the project as "no longer intact." The indecent exposure charges were dropped.

Peterson followed the Wischnatau controversy by winning several competitions and commissions in which he began to refine a style so restrained that some critics have suggested it borders on absence. In response to a call for designs for a visitor's center in a woodlands area outside Eugene, Oregon, Peterson's submission consisted of a single panel of clear glass adorned with nothing but the words "No public restrooms" etched in small print in a bottom corner. Though he won the competition, officials changed the panel's phrase to "Welcome to the Natural World" and placed an asphalt parking lot nearby. Peterson claimed the changes destroyed the integrity of the project. When the glass panel was mysteriously shattered only a year later, many suspected Peterson himself of the crime. He has offered no official comment on the destruction of the project other than its listing on his website as "No longer intact."

A similar project for the state of Washington ended in yet another lawsuit when Peterson set a four-room Department of Forestry administration building below ground level and then, upon its completion, covered it with earth, without any visible entrance.

"The building is about the role of governmental bureaucracy in the administration of natural beauty," Peterson said during a subsequent court proceeding. "The building was constructed according to plan and is on the agreed site. It's ready for use. And when the state digs their way down to it, could someone please apologize to the receptionist?"

The state did eventually unearth the building, but claimed it was damaged beyond repair. No one was found inside.

As a child, Peterson refused, to his mother's great consternation, to eat meat for three straight years. The non-meat phase ended one day when Peterson's mother saw him chase down a neighbor's chicken, wring its neck, and bring it to her with the demand that she prepare it for dinner. When she demanded an explanation of his actions, especially in light of his dietary beliefs, Peterson told his mother, "It looked at me."

Peterson underwent yet another messy public divorce in which his second wife claimed she suffered forced transvestitism and sexual abuse at Petersons' hands, and was at times held against her will. A particularly lascivious section of the trial transcript reads, "There was a three week period in which he spoke to me about nothing but anal sex, which I'd refused to have with him. When I tried to leave one evening, I found that all the doors were locked from the outside. Nathan pretended it was the result of a mix-up with a locksmith, but he was walking around naked and erect the entire evening, and finally I just gave in. Once he unlocked the doors the next morning, I left and never went back, though he kept claiming it was all just a misunderstanding."

"I've never forced anyone to do anything," Peterson said in the same trial. "I just seem to bring out the worst in people. I still feel I'll find the right person eventually."

Peterson's website lists The Beatles as his favorite band, their hit "All You Need is Love" as his favorite song.

The settlements from the divorce and the Washington Department of Forestry suit forced Peterson and Lothario to file for personal and corporate bankruptcy, respectively. Financial difficulties didn't stop Peterson from simultaneously creating two new firms, though, which he named FrontDoor and BackDoor. Both firms have thrived.

FrontDoor earned immediate acclaim for its construction of five Greyhound Bus Station terminals across Iowa and Nebraska, each of them a grouping of boxy, undersized glass buildings Peterson claims were inspired by phone booths. The firm is currently at work constructing a massive wastewater treatment plant built entirely of steel and glass in Rio de Janeiro.

BackDoor's first major project was the massive "Mall of the Rockies" in Denver, Colorado. In a move recalling the visitor's center in Washington, Peterson placed the entire structure underground, with parking at ground level directly over the mall. Peterson claimed the project would eventually be seen as the first "true late-capitalist structure."

"The American citizen consumes to escape reality," he wrote of the project. "As an increasingly harsh reality requires increasingly extreme consumption, the American mall functions primarily as a locale of obesity. As such, consumers and their malls find comfort in an opportunity to hide their embarrassing girth somewhere beneath the banal utility and damaging behavior that constitute the mundane, the 'everyday.'"

Though the finished structure appears from the outside to be nothing but a large concrete parking lot, critics agreed that the project managed to marry utilitarian function with political statement.

BackDoor has since won commissions to build Schools of Business on three major university campuses, and Peterson has pledged to use the projects to extend the ideas he developed while building the Mall of the Rockies.

"Everyone clever enough to major in business will have the opportunity to spend the majority of their time underground, drastically reducing their need to mix with the messier liberal elements of campus life," Peterson said in a recent interview.

Over the course of two years, while Peterson was in his early teens, a dozen cats disappeared from the neighborhood he lived in. After his family moved across town, five cats disappeared from the new neighborhood. When his father asked him if he knew anything about the missing cats, Peterson responded, "Why would I mess with cats? I don't even like cats."

Despite the architectural successes of FrontDoor and BackDoor, Peterson has continued to be pursued by scandal. Various entities have accused Peterson of using his firms to funnel and transfer funds illegally, hide assets, and generally confuse the details of his finances.

"When he needs to pretend to have access to millions of dollars, he can make it appear that he does, and then when he needs to look broke, he can make it look like he is," Washington state attorney general Richard Haslip said recently. According to Haslip, Peterson has yet to make payment on his legal settlement with the state.

"Bitter experience has taught me that access is not the same as ownership," Peterson responded.

In *Necropolis*, Peterson's most recent collection of theoretical essays, he writes that modern architecture's task is "to create habitations for dead people—people who are morally dead, spiritually dead, and actually dead. The world ended some time ago and the possibilities for the human race dissolved, but people are still animate and wandering the landscape, using their cell phones to take low quality pictures of nothing, which they then send to everyone they know. Contemporary architecture is about designing buildings that this new breed of dead human will never notice. Architecture's responsibility to human functionality is finished, and form without function is pointless. The result is that architecture, like the humanity that invented it and then promptly turned its back, is now a rotting corpse that doesn't know when to lie down."

"Church," one of American architect Nathan Peterson's recent structures, explores "implications inherent in the vacuity of the religious gesture," according to the architect. (Photo courtesy Church of the Testament, Duluth, Minn.)

This stance, which some critics have branded Peterson's "architecture of nihilism," has informed many of Peterson's newer structures, the most recent being a church he designed for a Protestant congregation in Duluth, Minnesota. Composed of shining metal and glass on the outside, Peterson left the concrete interior unfinished and even unplumbed. Peterson's website lists the project simply as "Church" and its goal as "exploring the structural implications inherent in the vacuity of the religious gesture."

"We had to scramble a bit, sure," the congregation's pastor said. "We hired a plumber, brought in some pews and chairs ourselves. It's a nice building, really, once we took care of those details."

"There's no point to being alive today," Peterson concluded in his statement from Lucerne. "I keep designing buildings mostly because the act has tremendous destructive potential—I destroy and clear out what was there before, and then replace it with something I know will soon be destroyed by someone else. The modern cycle of redundant carnage is invigorating. Eventually I'd like to tear down an entire small city and then not build anything in its place."

Acacia Avenue

We had just finished lunch and Jansen was still drinking a second highball when he looked out the plate glass window across the restaurant and told me he had been moved by buildings. "I know it's an odd thing to say, *moved by buildings*," he said, "and I don't know that I've ever said it out loud before. But through the window across the room I've been watching the side of a building I know nearby. I can only see a section of its west side through the branches of that tree, but that section has changed dramatically over the last ten minutes. I mention it as a way of apologizing if I've seemed distracted—though I suppose I also think you might understand."

Lunch that day was the first time I had seen Jansen in over forty years. By *understand*, then, he referred either to my career in urban planning, in which I've evaluated the relative merits of thousands of real and proposed structures while building one of the largest urban planning consulting firms on the east coast over the last few decades, or to the fact that Jansen and I had been roommates and friends while attending a prestigious liberal arts college in Portland, Oregon, in the late 1950s, and that somehow that bond had held, and there we were, eating lunch together in the twenty-first century. I followed Jansen's gaze out the window to a five-story building a few blocks away that loomed over the smaller one- and two-story structures that filled the rest of the neighborhood. "The brick apartment building?" I asked.

"It's been raining most of the time we've been here," he said, nodding. "But ten minutes ago the sun broke through and hit the side of the building. See how the brick looks almost impossibly red?"

"Like a stage set."

"But it's real. The brick is actually that red. I noticed it while you were talking about your brother. When I see a building like that, especially in the low-angle sunlight we get in the afternoon this time of year, it reminds me of a person facing a sunset, the way that last daylight flatters human features. So while we've been talking, I've had a sense that four blocks away that building is waking up—as if it's on the verge of speaking."

I told him it looked like a nice building. "They don't make them that way anymore," I said, and Jansen agreed that no, they didn't.

I had gone on to further degrees after college, and spent the intervening decades on the East Coast in pursuit of career success in the cities and family life in their suburbs. Jansen, however, had followed a different path. From what I understood, his family had been wealthy, and he had never held what most people would consider a real job. He had never married, never had any children, never, in fact, lived anywhere other than Portland. We had maintained minimal contact over the decades, primarily through Christmas gifts and cards Jansen sent every year, in which he never failed to ask by name about my wife and children. I, on the other hand, relied on my wife to take care of social niceties at the holidays. Jansen was never anything but a name on an envelope to her, so we often forgot to send him a gift at all, and would mail only a friendly but cursory thank you note some time after New Year's—and some years I forgot to send even that. When the next Christmas came around, though, there would be the card from Jansen again, accompanied by a tasteful gift: one year it was a leather-bound notebook, another a fountain pen, but most often it was simply a bottle of Veuve Clicquot. The champagne's cheerful orange label now reminds me of my family's Christmas dinners, in fact, because so many of those dinners ended with a round of champagne poured from the bottle Jansen had sent us.

But my wife divorced me and moved to California with a real estate developer in the late 1990's, and my children were grown and on their own. So that fall, when I learned that my father was dying of cancer, I took a leave of absence from work and returned to Portland to take care of him with my younger brother, Paul, who still lived and worked in one of Portland's suburbs. Even with the help of hospice nurses, caring for my father was intense and exhausting. But since a nurse was there during the day and Paul often drove in after work to pass the evening, I also had long, shapeless stretches of free time that soon began to wear on me as heavily as anything else. At first I checked in daily with my secretary, Dorothy, who has been with me for almost two decades now and who could probably run the firm on her own. She said she knew I was concerned that some of the ambitious junior partners might attempt to take control of the projects I was particularly interested in, and that she had already stymied those projects' progress in my absence by devising several distracting procedural and bureaucratic knots that the staff was too busy untangling to make any further advances. Eventually, after a week of my calls, she asked if I could please stop pestering her with advice. "We miss you," she assured me, "and we look forward to your return. But I'm sure there are plenty of things for you to deal with where you are right now, so don't worry about us." I spent the next two weeks in a state of aimless disconnection, the formless days floating slowly past, until finally I called Jansen and arranged our lunch meeting.

We reminisced about college, of course, but also spoke about our lives in general, especially the ways in which the places we'd lived had changed over the decades. Due to his family's long history of influence in Portland, Jansen was interested in many of the urban growth issues I'd wrestled with professionally over the years. Though he didn't have any formal education in urban planning, I was glad to find someone I could talk to about things that touched on what I felt was my other, more successful life back East—a life that had already, in only those few weeks I had been absent from it, begun to seem less real. It was as if the lion's share of my lifetime—marriage, parenthood, and career—had become nothing but a convincingly vivid dream that had dissolved to traces and shadows as each day I awakened to find myself not just in my family's old house, but in my parents' old room, since my bedridden and seemingly ancient father was confined to a first-floor bedroom that had once belonged to Paul and me. It was the same bedroom my mother had died in two decades earlier, amid a saccharine odor of disinfectant and decay that was immediately recognizable when it once again suffused the room all these years later. Neither Paul nor I mentioned the odor, though I'm sure we were equally disturbed by it, as we were by the unavoidable recognition that he and I were both old now too, and drinking too much in the evenings—probably more than was safe before Paul drove home after the late news.

I wasn't especially eager to return home from my lunch with Jansen, then. We lingered after finishing our meal, and he continued talking about buildings.

"I could tell you about most of the buildings in this neighborhood," he said after our plates had been cleared. "When they were built, by whom, what they were intended for, what they've been used for. I sometimes even catch myself referring to businesses that don't exist anymore. When giving directions, for instance, I can't seem to wrap my brain around the idea that Stanley's Drug is no longer on the corner down the street, to the extent that though I know the place is now one of those horrid Starbucks coffee shops, when I close my eyes and picture the intersection, I see modern SUV's driving past Stanley's Drug, and through the windows of the shop I can see Ted Stanley in his white dress shirt and tie, straightening the shelves or helping a customer who has come in looking for a bottle of camphor or maybe some iodine. I can see Ted and the customer and the iodine quite clearly, despite the fact that I know perfectly well that Ted died of a heart attack in the back room of that store over twenty years ago." Jansen closed his eyes a moment, as if lingering over his impossible image, and then smiled as he opened them. "It's odd, living your whole life in one place."

"You see every change," I said.

"But time passes strangely, so the changes become hazy, almost trivial. That there's a business called Starbucks down the street is just a dead fact. Stanley's Drug is so much more vibrant to me, though it predates most of the people who live here now."

It was odd for me to look across the table at Jansen as he sat there in his starched white dress shirt and checked gold tie, with his Mercury dime cufflinks just visible beyond the sleeves of a navy blue suit that, when I'd complimented him on it, he'd dismissed as "a department store outfit." I knew perfectly well how old we were, and that time had had its way with us, as it does with everyone. But I had grown old imperceptibly in my mirror over the years: it took twenty years for my hair to complete its process of thinning, receding, and going gray; the deepest wrinkles in my face had started years earlier as innocent sleep lines that faded by the time I finished breakfast; and my nose and ears were only just beginning to grow noticeably oversized in the way they are in the elderly. I had been back to Portland, on the other hand, for only brief visits every few years, and had never called Jansen. He'd never sent any photos with his Christmas cards, so even after decades, I had continued to picture the sender of my Christmas champagne as an awkward twenty-one-year-old student. From my perspective, then, he had aged forty years at once that afternoon.

While Jansen was in the bathroom, our waiter, a boy with deliberately mussed hair and a tattoo of Gothic lettering rising from beneath the side of his shirt collar, came to take away our empty glasses. "You just have to stand up and leave," he said. "Or he'll keep talking all day."

"You've had problems?" I said.

"No, but he doesn't tip. And he can be a real asshole if you say the wrong thing. No offense." He took the glasses and disappeared into the kitchen.

When Jansen came back and sat down, he looked at the empty white tablecloth between us. "Do you mind if we have one more round?" he asked.

After that round, I paid for lunch, tipped ten percent, and at Jansen's suggestion we went for a walk in the direction of the apartment building. He told me that though we were still too far from the building to tell, the cornices and a decorative line of trim were granite, there were two carved limestone corner braces in the shape of sirens, and a granite bust of Odysseus occupied a recessed spot over the entryway. I told him it sounded pretty ornate for an apartment building.

"It was originally a hotel," he said. "There was a time when there were plans to put a convention center in this neighborhood. One of the property owners wanted to get a jump on the business, so he built a hotel right away. But then the depression hit, and the convention center project was suspended."

"And the code must have been changed," I said. "None of the other buildings are the same height."

"It's a landmark to defeat at the hands of circumstance," Jansen said. "And now the convention center is on the other side of the river, with two hideous functionless towers that look like abandoned scaffolding."

We walked upon a slick surface of wet leaves that littered

the sidewalk. Jansen's steps were slow and deliberate, and I found myself watching our feet, the ponderous, halting rhythm of our shoes moving over the riotous colors and shapes beneath them: the spectacular yellow, copper, and ochre leaves, some like fallen stars, others like outspread hands, many torn, crushed, or otherwise destroyed as they lay there clogging the streets' gutters and drains.

I was tired by the time we reached the apartment building, and ready to be done with Jansen. I dutifully looked up at the corner braces on either side of the small entry courtyard, however, and studied the bust over the door, admitting that they were skillfully done.

"The sculptor was classically trained," Jansen said.

"The sirens' mouths are open," I said.

"Singing. Pretentious, no?"

"Out of context, at least."

"They thought people from all over the country would walk these streets," he said. "Maybe people from across the world. There were going to be restaurants and clubs and banks and shopping."

"Odysseus has ropes across his chest."

"Tied to the mast. So he can hear the song without chasing them."

"The building is the ship," I realized.

Jansen nodded. "Lindbergh had crossed the Atlantic. The world's fairs had huge exhibitions of technology and art. It's a shame," he said, raising his arm in a gesture that encompassed the entirety of the building. Many of the windows were cracked or broken and had been patched with tape or newspapers. The shrubs along the base were in need of trimming—castoff fast-food bags were impaled in some of the branches, and paper cups and cigarettes littered the ground.

"It's not being maintained," I said.

"There's no need," Jansen said. "Because three months from now, it won't be here. They're tearing it down, along with these smaller buildings on either side. They want to put in glassy little boxes with stores at the street level and overpriced condos above."

The misting rain had grown thicker as we stood there—it dripped from the brim of Jansen's hat and darkened the shoulders of his raincoat as I remarked that though the loss of the building was unfortunate, the new development might be an improvement for the neighborhood as a whole.

"Do you see the siren to the right, the one closest to us?" he asked.

I looked up—the woman's face was framed in garlands of long, wavy hair. The surface of the stone was pitted in a way common to weathered sandstone, and the point beneath the chin where rain dripped was stained a greenish-yellow. Though her eyes were the smooth, pupil-less crescents that so many statues possess and which always strike me as indicating blindness, the face was slightly upturned, as if she were singing to the sky. "The more attractive of the two," I said.

"I've always thought so," Jansen said. "Because that's my mother."

I looked at Jansen, and then back at the figure. There was no resemblance between the old man and the young woman.

"She was the model," he said. "I was just a small child, but I can still remember it, the excitement my family felt when we came to see the building when it was done. We used to have a photo from that day, of my mother standing in front of the building, smiling. But that's been lost a long time ago."

I didn't know what to say. Water fell from the siren's chin in small drops that disappeared in the mist.

"So I was glad when you called and asked about lunch," Jansen said. "I thought maybe you could help me."

"I don't know anything about the way things are done here," I told him.

"But you know how it works in general," he said. "I don't expect you to be an expert or a savior—just someone to help me understand."

I told Jansen I would help him however I could—to offer anything less at that point would have been impossibly callous. Over the next half hour, he told me more about the city's plans: the entire neighborhood had been targeted for reclamation, it seemed, and the city was eager to start its process of "enhancing livability." In my experience that usually involves getting rid of minorities, and I noted that while Jansen and I stood there talking, the only people I saw entering or exiting the apartment building were black or Hispanic women, many with small children. Most eyed us warily as they passed.

Jansen and I parted ways after I agreed to attend a planning commission meeting with him the next week, and as I drove home to relieve the hospice nurse, I tried to remember what I could of Jansen's family. He had rarely gone home while we were in college, despite the fact that we were only twenty minutes from his parents' house. In fact, he almost never left our dorm room or, later, our university-owned apartment. He had spent almost all of his evenings and weekends studying, though I couldn't remember what he'd majored in—it might have been history, I thought. He'd never gone to parties, and I remembered that other students had known him primarily for his knowledge of Homer. He could recite long passages of the *Iliad* by memory, and had helped numerous boys in our hall study for their world literature course freshman year, offering impromptu tutoring sessions at the small desk in the corner of our dorm room, where he explained the subtler aspects of the relationships among the Greeks. I also remembered that Jansen's perpetual presence in our room had become an especially sore point between us during a period in which I'd had a girlfriend and had hoped for a private place to take her at the end of a date. Jansen had refused to leave our room, saying he would have nowhere else to go—a ridiculous claim to make when I knew perfectly well that his family lived just across town. I remembered being angry with him when the girl broke up with me for a boy who had his own car and a more obliging roommate. That had all been so long ago, though, that the entire period had been compressed to but a flicker of memory, and the girl to only a sketch. The next time I saw Jansen, I decided, I would at least ask him what his major had been.

Later that night, after Paul and I had our whiskey-and-sevens at the kitchen table and he had gone home, I went to look in on my father. I was surprised to find that he had managed to shift himself into a sitting position, his back against the headboard—the movement must have cost him tremendous effort. "Dad?" I said. "Are you awake?"

He turned slowly toward me. Even in his dark room, the faint pink glow of a nearby streetlight cast enough light through the window for me to see that his eyes were open. "You remember what your mother looked like, don't you?" he asked.

"Of course," I said.

His eyes wandered the room. "She was very small," he said. "She would put her fingers on my face. On my eyes."

"You should sleep, Dad."

"She never blamed me," he said. "I don't know why."

"You're tired, Dad. Get some rest."

"Did you know that? I don't think you did. You left—you were never here." He looked at me for a long time without saying anything, his eyes faint, watery reflections in the dark, and I wondered if he was trying to start one of our old arguments again. But then he raised his head suddenly, as if startled. "You're not alone, are you?" he said. "Who's with you?"

His flare-ups of paranoid confusion had been occurring with increasing regularity. "There's no one else," I assured him. "It's just me."

"Someone's with you. There has to be," he shouted, clutching at his blankets. "Who were you talking to? Where are they?" He began tearing the blankets from himself, and when I moved to stop him, he flailed his arms wildly. Before I could restrain him, one of his elbows caught me just above the eyebrow. The blow stunned me at first, but the angry surge of pain helped me focus, and I soon held his arms in a vise grip at his sides. I growled at him to calm down as I lay awkwardly across his chest and held him while he emitted strange, desperate yelps. The bed was equipped with restraints, but as I tried to formulate a strategy for getting to them I felt his body grow slack beneath mine. His chest heaved as he sobbed wordlessly in my ear. "You're exhausted," I said as I let go of him and stood up. "You need to sleep." When I moved to the light switch and turned it on, I saw my father there in his bed, crying silently beneath white sheets dotted with bright red stains. I put my fingers to my eyebrow and they came away wet with blood. "I'm wounded," I said, laughing. I examined myself in the mirror that hung behind his door: a straight red gash along the outside of my eyebrow bled healthily and was beginning to swell. Breathless and sweaty, I looked like a boxer who'd gotten the worse end of a fight. "You just beat me up," I said, but my father gave no sign of hearing. I went down the hall to the bathroom to clean and dress the wound, and when I returned, my father was slumped against his headboard. Though I could hear and see him breathing, I placed my fingers on his neck anyway—his pulse was fine, and I moved him down into the bed and fixed his blankets. When I saw him the next morning and asked him if he remembered hitting me, he stared at me blankly. "I would never in my life hit a child," he said.

A week later, the cut above my eye concealed beneath a Band-Aid, I went with Jansen to the planning commission meeting scheduled at a nearby community center. When we stepped into the lobby, however, we found ourselves amid a surprising crowd of families, many with outrageously dressed children. The stench of standing water filled the air, and one of the mothers informed us that the basement had flooded. A children's theater production of *Peter Pan* scheduled for that evening had been completely washed out, it seemed, as sets, props, and costumes stored in the basement were underwater and unsalvageable. Many of the wildly dressed children in the lobby—various Lost Boys and Girls who had been eager to make their debuts—were crying.

Amid the confusion, Jansen and I eventually found someone who told us the planning commission meeting had been moved to the west side of the city. Jansen didn't drive after sundown anymore, and since I wasn't eager to negotiate unfamiliar areas at night in the rain, we took a light rail train to the meeting, arriving in time to listen to citizens make angry statements about an issue involving the fencing and possible covering of a reservoir in a city park. The topic of Jansen's building didn't come up for another hour, and when the development including Jansen's building was finally opened for discussion, Jansen betrayed no outward sign of interest other than a compulsive plucking at the thighs of his wool slacks. Only one person stepped to the microphone, a small man our age dressed in a suit whose cut was at least twenty years out of style. He coughed nervously and adjusted his bifocals as he read a formal speech regarding the need to name the apartments a historical building. After one of the commissioners explained that placing the building on a register of historic places could have been done years previously, and supposed there must have been a reason it hadn't happened, the man at the microphone laughed nervously. "I think, Mister Commissioner, that perhaps it was because there were a number of years that the building was known for catering to unseemly sorts of people. And maybe the owners weren't especially seemly themselves." A titter of laughter passed through the room, and though the man at the microphone blushed, he seemed to warm to the attention. "There were a lot of ladies of the evening there, you know, so maybe people weren't especially interested in the building at that time, sir." The commissioners and the man at the microphone traded a few insinuating comments about interest in the building until eventually the man thanked them, stepped away, and the meeting moved to other topics.

As we sat next to each other on the train back downtown, Jansen asked what I had thought. I told him it seemed to me the project was only the latest in a string of strategic changes, and because the timing of the projects had been planned long ago, it was unlikely the city was going to allow one link in the chain to fail. The apartment building had probably been picked for demolition for the exact reasons the man at the meeting had defended it: it had a disreputable past and wasn't historically protected, making it more affordable for the developers who had purchased it. It sounded as if the destruction of the building would raise no more protest than what we had seen that night. "If you want to stop it, it's really a legal issue," I told him. "You should hire a lawyer and get him to start filing motions and injunctions, and then get the media involved. Find the architect who designed the building, or original tenants in a sentimental mood, or claim the sculptures are part of an important stage in the development of the artist who made them, and if the guy's not alive anymore, find surviving relatives and get them to plead. Tonight's meeting was just a rubber stamp in a bureaucratic process."

Jansen shook his head as he looked into the darkness rushing past the windows of the train, a void broken only by the occasional smear of a passing light or, when the tracks ran briefly along the highway, refracted strings of headlights. "The sculptor had no family," he said. "And I've never been a fan of the media."

"No one's a fan of the media," I said. "I'm just giving you options."

"And I thank you for that. They just don't appeal to me right now."

"Well, continuing to do nothing will achieve nothing," I said, attempting a ridiculously casual shrug to cover my frustration. "You can attend every meeting, but if you don't say anything, the last event you'll attend will be the razing of the building."

"I'm sorry," Jansen said, touching me above the elbow—an oddly effective conciliatory gesture. "I've made you angry."

"I just don't know what you want me to do."

He looked out the window of the train again, into a surprisingly open looking stretch of hills and trees visible primarily as shadows huddled at the margins of light coming from a few scattered houses. "All of this used to be farmland when we graduated from college," he said. "I used to drive out here and sketch the trees and hills and the dirt roads that cut through them. You'd gone off to graduate school back East, but I wasn't sure what I wanted to do with my life—the choice of a job at that point seemed like an irreversible life decision. So I moved back in with my parents, though I was embarrassed about it, because it seemed like a step backward. I started waking up and leaving as early as possible, driving out of the city and onto random country roads until I found a stand of trees or an old barn or creek that struck me in some way, and I'd sketch the scenery until lunch, which I brought along in a paper bag. I spent the afternoons napping in the car, or reading, or just driving around. But the person I would show my sketches to, who was helping me with my drawing in whatever vague way I was working on it at that time, was the same person who did the sculptures on the building."

"He'd kept in contact?"

"He was a kind of family friend—and had been for as long as I could remember. His name was Claude Grimmel. He was a painter and sculptor, and for a number of years he'd rented a garage and storage space along the outfitting store my father owned, which is where I brought my sketches to him. He was a rail thin man who smoked constantly. I can still remember the smell of his cigarettes in that garage, and the way he could never sit still. My father had a small shooting range at the back of the building, where customers were allowed to test-fire guns or rifles that were for sale. So when Grimmel was studying my sketches and I was standing there watching him, it wasn't unusual to hear gunshots. They always startled him, and his arms would jump in the sleeves of his white dress shirts like he was a marionette. He used to keep his shirt cuffs unbuttoned, and they would be stained black by the charcoal he sketched with, so these dark circles at the ends of his arms would jump when Grimmel jumped, and he would make a face like he'd been shot himself, and then pace around and roll his neck like he needed to recover from the shock while he muttered about how my father had told him the shooting range would hardly ever be used. He looked closely at my drawings, though, and encouraged me. He said that if I continued to work, he was confident something would come of it. That sounded fine to me, though I don't suppose I had any idea what that something would be."

Our train was moving back into downtown Portland by then, making stops every few minutes. It was late on a weeknight, so there had been a number of stops at which the doors had slid open to reveal no one waiting to board. The doors would stand open, however, as if anticipating the arrival of some absent passenger, until finally, when the pointlessness of the mechanical gesture had become almost ridiculous, a female voice would announce, "The doors...are closing," and they would rumble shut, hissing as they suctioned together and locked.

"One day a couple months into this routine," Jansen continued, "my mother came to Grimmel's studio with me. She wanted to see some of my sketches, she said. I kept my work hidden when I was at home, because my father was against the way I was spending my time, and I didn't want him to see any evidence that would further fuel his theories about me *wasting my youth*, as he liked to say. I wasn't pleased with the sketches I was bringing in that day, I remember, and I wished that my mother had chosen a different day to visit, but Grimmel looked at them and said the same things to my mother that he had said to me: that the sketches showed talent, and if I developed that talent, something would come of it. My mother said that was wonderful, and began telling Grimmel something preposterous about how she always knew I had a good eye, and they spent the next several minutes discussing me through a series of more and more general comments, until it was as if they were no longer discussing me at all, but instead discussing the abstract idea of a person, and all the things this hypothetical person possibly could or would do. As I listened to their increasingly baroque discussion, and watched the way my mother stood directly across from Grimmel, tucking and retucking the same loose strand of hair behind her ear, I noticed how the two of them looked only at each other and never at my work, how they laughed at each other's comments but never addressed me, and how Grimmel, for the first time I could ever remember, seemed at ease. I realized that for Grimmel and my mother it was as if I wasn't even in the room—they had completely ceased to notice me, even though they were discussing my work and I was right there, just a few feet away."

The train had stopped across from the city's minor league baseball stadium, a structure whose uppermost level of seating was even with the street and divided from the sidewalk by a high fence of closely spaced iron bars. When the train doors opened again to an empty platform, I could see directly across the street to the fence, and I was struck by the way the seats descended immediately beyond the barrier, making it appear that if someone were to scale the fence and leap off the other side, they would plunge down into the stadium the way a person plunges from a cliff. "The doors...are closing," the woman's voice reported again, and the scene was then reduced to just a handful of iron bars framed in the black rubber that bordered the door's slim windows. Then the train lurched into motion, and even that image rolled away.

"I suppose," Jansen said, "that I knew that my mother and Grimmel had been carrying on. I had no direct knowledge, of course, but all of the circumstances pointed to it: something about the nature of the modeling she had done for him, and the strange way that if his name ever came up in conversation she pretended hardly to know him. And of course the idea for Grimmel to work with me on my drawing had been my mother's in the first place, a suggestion she gave me the first time I admitted to her how I'd been putting so many miles on the car that was supposedly hers, but which she never drove. So even the fact that I was there in Grimmel's studio was the result of a transaction involving my mother. It was as if my life had somehow slipped into a closed system, some circle of influence that revolved around Grimmel and my mother and from which I couldn't escape, and I remember how as I stood there listening to Grimmel compliment my work, and as I watched the way he and my mother looked at each other, that in that moment my entire project, however hazy or ill-defined it was, seemed to dissolve before my eyes, and I looked at my sketches spread out on the table and at some older ones Grimmel had taped to the wall, and I saw, I really saw, that the drawings were absolutely pedestrian, and that I had no real ability, that nothing could ever possibly come of my work, and that despite the fact that I was in my twenties, I was still just a boy, really—a tiny, confused bit of a huge world I still had no experience in and couldn't possibly understand. I felt this so powerfully as my mother and I left Grimmel's studio that day that I made sure to take all of my work with me, and when we returned home and my mother went up to her bedroom, I gathered all of my drawings, every scrap of paper on which I'd penciled even the smallest figure or marginal shape, and I tore them into small pieces that I carried into our living room, where I built a fire in the fireplace and then fed the scraps of paper into it until every one of them was gone. I took my drawing supplies—all my pencils, erasers, pads, and loose paper, my charcoals, everything I'd taken with me on my drives—and carried them out to our trash bin, and lifted the bag that was on top, and dropped my supplies into the bin, and then set the bag back down on top of them so that they couldn't be seen. And then I went back into the house, and I was done with drawing.

"That evening, I found my father in his study, and I asked him if there were any possibility of his finding me a job at his store. He was surprised, and despite all the times he'd claimed I should find a real job, he said he thought I was working on my drawing. Despite his scorn for what I was doing, it seemed he also understood that it was the result of something fundamental in my character and not just an idle curiosity I could somehow ignore. I was still upset about what had happened that day, though, and I blurted out something about how after working with Grimmel for a bit, I'd decided that Mother and Grimmel were both artistic, and we didn't need any more artists around. My father stiffened immediately—it was almost as if even his pulse and breathing had stopped. 'You've been working with Claude?' he asked, upon which I realized that because I never actually passed through the store part of the building when I went to Grimmel's studio, my father had no idea I'd been visiting Grimmel, and that I'd known, really, that my mother wouldn't have told him, and that what I'd just said was somehow a violation not of any specific secret, but of a more general, unspoken code of silence whereby Grimmel and my mother, in the years since the apartment building had been completed, were just not to be mentioned together. I told my father that yes, I'd been showing Grimmel some of my work, but that I'd decided to stop, and my father shifted in his chair and rearranged some of the things on his desk, and our conversation moved on to some generic discussion of positions he might have at the store. But the next morning, he didn't once refer to our conversation of the previous evening, nor did he the day after that—in fact, neither of us ever spoke of it again, not only about myself or my mother and Grimmel, but also about my father helping me find a job. I can only assume that I had accidentally linked those two subjects as one and the same, and though my father might eventually have spoken about a job, the silence on the subjects became terribly permanent when only three weeks later I read in the newspaper that some hikers had found Grimmel's body in a shallow creek in the hills outside of town, and that he had been bound hand and foot, the newspaper said, and beaten about the head and torso, and shot twice in the chest."

The train rolled to a halt at our stop, and when the doors opened, Jansen and I stepped into the cold, wet night. The rain had stopped, and we were able to walk away from the train without opening our umbrellas, leaving the recorded female voice to bid us goodnight with her eversame warning, though the damp air muted her voice. The train whined to life and rolled away behind us as we moved down the street.

"You make it sound as if your father killed Grimmel," I said.

"It's a logical conclusion," Jansen said. "But it didn't even occur to me at the time, and I still can't believe he would have been capable of something like that. My father lived either in front of the black and white television in our living room or behind the oak desk in his study. How could I possibly picture him beating and shooting people in the wilderness? He didn't attend Grimmel's funeral, though, because he claimed he wasn't able to leave work that day. So I escorted my mother to the funeral alone. It was a small, brief event, throughout which my mother maintained complete silence. But it must have been during roughly those same weeks that my father moved a cot into his study under the pretense that he had the flu and didn't want my mother to catch it, though even after he recovered he kept sleeping in his study, and we were changed into the equivalent of boarders living beneath the same roof: my father in his study, my mother in her bedroom, and me in the living room, where I would sit and read for hours at a time."

"Was anyone ever caught?"

"No, but I wasn't paying much attention to those events, so I'm not sure where the investigation stalled. Though I'd taken my drawings to Grimmel, I hadn't been close to him. In fact, I suppose I vaguely disliked him, and his death struck me as a novelty—he was the first person I knew who had been murdered. Looking back on it now, though, it was really his death that set in place a pattern that remained unchanged in my family for the rest of my parents' lives. Other than a short, quiet dinner each evening, my father kept to his study, my mother lived upstairs in her room, and I took over the rest of the house, which I soon came to think of as *my* house, though neither my mother nor father passed away for another twenty years."

"You lived there the entire time?" I said.

"You didn't notice?"

"I didn't come back very often. And I was so busy when I did that I never had a chance to look you up."

Jansen smiled as if embarrassed by some small faux pas. "I mean the Christmas gifts," he said. "The return address on them would always have been the same: 837 Acacia Avenue."

After Jansen and I parted and I drove home, I was surprised to find my brother's car still parked in front of our house, and was even more surprised when I entered the kitchen door and heard the voices of my brother and father engaged in clear, lucid conversation—my father's voice, especially, seemed to have lost the raggedness I'd grown used to, its guttural, confused rambling. I felt as if fifty years had dropped away as easily as a curtain falls, and I was a teenager again returning home from a night out as I walked down the dark hallway to the light coming from the bedroom, where I found Paul leaning forward intently in his chair as there in the bed my father sat straight up, as if he had no need of the pillows he was propped against. Though his eyes were bright and his head unbowed, his posture revealed the extent to which his body had been consumed by disease. His cheek bones protruded from his face, his chest was sunken beneath his pajamas, and his arms were almost nothing but bones covered with loose skin. But he was talking.

"Here he finally is," he said, smiling at me as I stepped into the room. "Isn't it past your curfew? I don't see a clock, but I bet if I did, you'd be in trouble."

I looked to Paul, who nodded eagerly. "Dad's talkative tonight," he said.

"Insomnia's got the best of me," my father said, "so I've been telling Paul here about the things we'll need to think about for Canada."

"For our trip to British Columbia, Tommy," Paul added. My brother hadn't called me "Tommy" since I'd graduated college, and I was completely baffled by the context of their remarks until I remembered that my father, brother, and I had gone camping in British Columbia during spring break the year I was a high school senior—the first and only time the three of us ever went on a trip without my mother. It had been years since I'd even thought about it.

"It'll be cold up there," my father said gravely. "We'll need to pack heavy—plenty of coats and scarves."

"But this is spring break, Dad," Paul said. "Isn't there any chance we'll get some sun, get to enjoy the beach?"

My father started to say something, but stopped, as if reconsidering. He looked at the two of us, his two sons, and it seemed as if he were passing through stages of uncertainty—as if each succeeding thought that presented itself to him was somehow equally confusing. I had the strange feeling, though, that what we were seeing was somehow the opposite of the medication-induced dementia my father had been suffering lately: instead of everyone and everything striking him as strange or alien, it seemed in those moments that he had returned to immediate reality, and realized that the two sons sitting in his room were both in their sixties, but that he'd been talking to them as if they were in their teens, and that the trip he was helping them prepare for had already occurred and been long forgotten, because he was actually in his late eighties and sitting in a strange bed in a bedroom that wasn't his own, while his old sons watched him with unconcealed and disconcerting fascination. Even though all of these impressions would have been accurate, they must also have been even more disorienting than any of his delusions, and he smiled and patted his covers nervously. "I think I'm feeling tired now, after all," he said. "Maybe I should try to get some sleep."

"We'll figure it out in the morning," Paul said as we helped our father lie down. He responded with an encouraging nod.

After my father was asleep, Paul and I sat at the kitchen table and had our usual glasses of whiskey. "For twenty minutes, he was absolutely there!" Paul said, elated. "He responded to everything I said, we had a normal conversation."

"In the wrong decade," I said.

"But at least he was fully present in that decade," Paul said. "I'll take that any day of the week."

After Paul left that night, I had another glass of whiskey and thought about how our actual trip to Canada had gone. It had poured rain for most of the four days, I remembered. Paul and I had tried to smuggle a six-pack of beer along in our sleeping bags, but my father had discovered and confiscated it when we were unpacking at the campsite. We thought we would have a manly few days of catching fish and cooking them over a fire, but we ended up spending most of our time wet and cold, playing cards in our tent and eating uncooked hot dogs and cans of beans. Finally, on our last afternoon there, my father and I got into a shouting match over whether some wood I'd gathered was too wet to use in a fire. As was usual in those days, the shouting escalated into my father grabbing me by the jacket, and I tore his hands off me and pushed him away, then stomped off down the muddy camp road, getting deliberately soaked while I practiced an enraged speech I would never actually deliver. The long drive home passed in exhausted silence, and I took a hot shower and crawled into bed as soon as we got back. Paul and I shared the downstairs bedroom then, and my mother brought bowls of steaming soup to us that evening. "At least you made it back in one piece," she said.

I had fallen asleep at the kitchen table for a few minutes and awoke confused, staring dumbly at the open bottle of whiskey until I remembered where and when I was. I looked in on my father, and then climbed the stairs to his old room, where my things were. I slept soundly and awoke in the morning to sunlight that streamed in the window and illuminated a section of the floor in a blaze of varnish and dust. I felt grateful for the rest, and when I went downstairs and into my father's room, he lay exactly as he had the previous night. I'd thought his hair was white, but against the clean white sheet I could see that the long strands were clearly the faintly translucent blue-silver of ice, as were the distinct, wiry hairs on his arms and the stubble that dotted the pink skin beneath his sideburns and chin. Later, I would wonder at what point I realized my father was dead—it was certainly before I moved forward and felt his cold skin. I think I knew as soon as I stepped into the room, and maybe even as soon as the moment I woke up. And some hidden part of me certainly knew even before that.

After my father's body was taken away in an ambulance, I found myself in command of a sudden, cold rage, as if a spell had been broken, and I launched into unceasing vengeful action. I purchased the most expensive casket and marker primarily so I could shame the salesman by asking him if helping people price-shop the death of their loved ones was a truly gratifying career. When notifying family members, I used a viciously mocking irony to undercut every thoughtless cliché they sputtered at me from their end of the phone, including making one of my cousins cry by saying I wasn't sure how it was a blessing to be locked in a box six feet underground. And I went through everything in the house without an ounce of sentiment, deciding that I wanted to keep for myself exactly nothing that was there. I was aware that my behavior was appalling, and yet I found myself unable to act in any other way—some dark force of will had risen so powerfully within me that any attempt to deny it would have been futile. And though I didn't forget entirely about Jansen and his building, I felt absolutely freed from that concern, as if my father's death exempted me from all obligations or human connections.

So I was encouraged that when Jansen showed up at my father's wake—wearing the same suit he'd worn each time I'd seen him—he made no mention of his apartment building or the commission meeting. He looked haggard and unkempt, in fact—as if he either hadn't slept, or had slept badly and with his suit on—and he seemed to avoid me. He met my eyes only once, from across the room, with a look that I knew was more grief-stricken than the composed, almost business-like expression I was maintaining. When he finally made his way to where Paul and I stood, he solemnly shook not my hand, but Paul's, and made Paul promise to call him if he ever needed anything. "There's no easy way to lose a parent," he told Paul. "I went through a difficult period when my own father passed away, and there's no real comfort but time." As Jansen nodded in my direction and then departed, it took every bit of willpower I had to resist observing that this time that is supposedly comforting is the very thing that first maims and then kills us.

Jansen didn't come to the funeral the next day, and over the next week I pressed Paul to help me conclude our father's affairs as quickly as possible. I put off calling Jansen, even wondering whether it was really necessary for me to see him again. That question was settled, though, when he called one morning and, as if detecting the trend of my thoughts, said he wanted to be sure I would stop by to see him once more before I left.

I put it off until the last day—my bags were packed and in the trunk of the car when I parked along the curb in front of Jansen's house, a smallish old Victorian painted dark blue. When he opened the door and I stepped into the entryway, I told him I was sorry I couldn't stay long, but my flight was later that afternoon. He didn't respond to my apology, but instead promised a cup of tea as he led me down a short hall to the living room at the back of the house, from which he disappeared into an adjoining kitchen.

The living room was small. A love seat sat between two end tables along one wall, with a pine coffee table in front of them. Across from the love seat sat two small, royal blue armchairs with shiny spots on the armrests and seat cushions where the felt was worn. The wall beyond the seating arrangement held a small, floor-level fireplace in which the blackened remains of some burned logs still sat, and two rows of ceramic tile set in the fir floor formed the hearth. As I sat on the love seat and looked out into the brief backyard, where rhododendrons fought an overgrown olive tree for space, I realized that I had pictured the house incorrectly. The house I'd envisioned when Jansen spoke to me on the train never would have fit on this lot—I had imagined long hallways and expansive rooms without ceilings, as if Jansen's family had lived on the set of a soap opera. This house, with its simple rooms and basic layout, seemed perfectly adequate for one man to live in, but I could hardly picture the situation Jansen had described. His father's study must have been the alcove I saw just off the entryway, a room it had taken me only two strides to pass. There was no grand staircase to the upstairs bedroom—his mother must have walked up the short, straight staircase at the back of the house into a room that certainly had a low ceiling and dormer windows. I had pictured Jansen sitting upon a raised hearth as an immense, roaring fire virtually pulled his sketches from his fingertips, but now I saw that he would have had to kneel in front of the small fireplace and force his drawings almost directly into the flames themselves.

"So this was originally your parents' house?" I asked.

"My grandparents, actually," he answered from the kitchen. "My mother's father had it built. He was a banker—the source of the family wealth."

I knew bankers could do fine, but I had long ago stopped associating people that handled money with people who were wealthy. "So it's been handed down through the family," I said as he returned to the room with our cups of tea, which he placed carefully on the coffee table before settling into one of the armchairs.

"It's the only place I've ever lived, except for college, with you," he said. "What will you do with your own father's house? It's a nice old one—it would be a good place to live, if you wanted."

"Not for me," I said, laughing automatically and realizing my remark's implications only after I'd spoken. "It's nice, of course. But my business is back East."

"You could retire here, though."

"I don't believe in retirement," I said.

"Some work of noble note may yet be done?" he asked with a wry smile, as if it were an inside joke between us.

It annoyed me not just that I couldn't place the line, but that he would test me that way. I'm perfectly familiar and comfortable with pretension, but I can't stand a man who condescends to me, and I wanted to erase the smile from his face. "Is that Homer?" I asked.

"Tennyson," he said.

"Didn't you major in history?"

"Art history. I wrote my senior thesis on Guido Reni."

"I don't know who that is."

"Religious stuff, mostly. David and Goliath."

I was flooded by the desire to escape Jansen's oppressive, swirling existence as soon as possible, to find my way out of the city and never return. I thought of Dorothy sitting at her desk outside my office in her tan slacks and crisp white blouse, and the gray hair that she still kept long and often in a ponytail, as she answered the phone, handled paperwork, and arranged meetings, all with utter aplomb and supreme attention to detail. "I've never known much about that," I said.

"Not many do," Jansen said, studying the burned logs in the fireplace. "Ah, I almost forgot. I have something for you."

He left the room again, and I heard him walk down the hallway and open a door at the other end—presumably the study—and then there was silence. I stood and wandered toward the fireplace. The windows that gave onto the backyard were uncovered, and as I stood in the watery afternoon light that filtered through the olive branches and into the living room, I noticed how few things there were in the room. Built-in bookshelves flanked the fireplace, but the mantel above was bare, as were the walls. The surfaces of the floor and table were immaculate, and the hearth was unmarked by any soot stains or stray ashes. I thought again of my assumptions about the house, how I had pictured Jansen and his father and mother leading lonely, isolated lives within its walls, but how actually, with curtains on the windows sealing in the clutter of three adult lives, the environment would have been claustrophobic. No one would ever have been more than a wall or two away from anyone else. They would have been walking past one another almost constantly.

Jansen returned to the room and stood immediately next to me, shoulder to shoulder. He held in his hand an old black and white photo, which he raised so that we could both see it: I immediately recognized my father, brother, and I standing in our front yard, each of us holding a fishing rod. Instinctively, I snatched the photo from Jansen's hand and pushed him away. I didn't think I'd pushed him very hard, but he stumbled backward, and when his heel caught against the edge of the hearth, I realized he was going to fall. I felt myself, in that drawn-out moment, paralyzed by two immediate but contradictory urges: one part of me sought to reach for Jansen, while another desired to deliver some final blow that would finish him off. The result was that I remained motionless, looking on as if I were located somewhere outside of myself, struck by what I saw in Jansen's expression: he gazed placidly up at me as he fell, the muscles of his face relaxed, his lips parted—it was almost an expression of pleasure. He landed with a sudden exhalation on the hard tiles in front of the fireplace, falling first into a sitting position before his momentum rolled him onto his back. He groaned, but the groan quickly decayed into a tired laugh as he rolled to his side and pushed himself up.

"What is this?" I demanded, holding the picture.

"I'm sorry," he said, still laughing from where he sat on the floor. "It's ridiculous. You're lucky I didn't break something."

"Where is this from?"

"Your desk."

"What do you mean?"

"Help me up."

I offered him a hand, and as he pulled himself to his feet and began straightening and examining his clothing as if he were more worried about possible damage to his suit than to anything else, I looked at the photo again. My mother must have taken it to document the occasion of Paul and me having received the fishing gear—probably a Christmas morning—since I knew the three of us had only ever gone fishing together once, and probably never stood together like that again.

"I took things," Jansen said. "In college sometimes. Little things, when people weren't looking—scarves, key chains, small photos. I would feel guilty and want to give them back later, but how do you explain something like that? When you don't even understand it yourself?"

"You can keep it," I said.

"No," he said. "It's yours."

"Then why have you had it all these years?"

"I don't know!" he said, his voice rising. "Why didn't you ever call me, or write me? You didn't even know it was gone." He sighed as if exhausted, and placed his hand over his face. "This isn't the way I wanted this to go."

There was something theatrical about Jansen's fatigue, as well as his admission that there was a way he wanted things to go, some script he'd devised and from which he was sorry we'd deviated. "My life wasn't here anymore," I said. "What do you—"

"Don't," he said, raising his hand. "You don't have to explain. I'm just worn-out." He looked tiredly around the room as if everything in it exhausted and depressed him. "Do you ever feel like everything is over without anything ever having happened?" he said.

"Yes," I said. It was the first time in weeks that I didn't feel like attacking what someone had said.

He stepped to the table to retrieve his cup of tea, and when he turned back to me, he seemed also to have regained some of his composure. "We're not the same," he said. "I understand that. But I think I know you well, and that you know me too. I always followed your career, you know. I've been proud of what you've accomplished."

"It was just business."

"What isn't," he said, shrugging. "And I'm sorry if I wasted your time about that building. I'm not sure anything can really be done."

"It could be restored," I said.

He examined me as if trying to judge whether I was telling the truth. "Yes, I suppose it could," he said slowly. "But I should let you go."

"Are you sure you're alright?"

"Nothing a little whiskey won't cure." We headed down the hall to the front door, and after I stepped onto the porch, I turned to face him. I had no plans to ever return to Portland, and I'm sure he knew it. It was an overcast day, but he squinted as he peered toward the street, as if the world beyond his porch were unbearably bright. "Do you like the champagne?" he said.

"Yes," I said. "I always look for it."

"Then I'll send you more. This Christmas."

We shook hands, and I climbed into the car and drove to the airport, and my attention was occupied with the practical concerns of travel until I settled into my window seat on the plane. As we lifted off the runway, though, my thoughts returned again to my firm. It pleased me to think of my desk, the papers that would be stacked upon it, the messages I would have to sift through, and the projects I would need to be brought up to speed on. I was looking forward to getting back.

A bright, even light filled the cabin then, bathing the

faces of the passengers in a flattering glow, filling out their features—we had broken through the cloud cover and were rising above it, into clearer skies. At the appearance of the light, people raised their heads and looked to the windows, and passengers in the window seats began lowering the plastic shades. I continued looking out my own window for some time, though, gazing down into the crests of cloud that fell away below us. From above, the clouds stretched to the horizon in all directions, like a vast, slate-gray sea that one could never hope to cross.

Continuity

There were only two employees in the store when the man walked in. It was half an hour until closing on a Wednesday night. The headlights of night traffic swept past the storefront windows, diffracted in light rain. The store smelled of canvas, of soap, and of course of paint. The man glanced uncertainly at the different brands of paint, the cans stacked in clean and even rows. All of the labels faced forward and all of the handles fell to the back.

One of the employees, a young man in a baseball hat, was talking while he mopped a section of floor near the counter at back of the store, where there were cash registers and mixing machines. "So then later there's a car chase," he was saying, "and it's not a great car chase, but that's not important. It's a car chase that's supposed to be in New York, right? But then when one of the cars crashes and the cops get out, if you look in the background, there's this billboard on the side of a building. It's not in perfect focus because it's in the background, and it's only visible for a second, but you can still see the words on the billboard, and one of the words is *color*. Except that on the billboard it's spelled c-o-l-o-u-r, with that extra *u*."

"The British spelling," the other employee said. A thin, middle-aged man with close cut gray hair and glasses, he seemed like the manager. He tore a receipt from a cash register and studied it.

"Right," the younger employee said, "and you know why? Because it wasn't even New York. It's cheaper to film in Canada, so they use this Canadian city, but they call it New York. I think it was Toronto."

"Did you need some help?" the manager asked.

"I'm just looking for a flat paint," the customer said. "For interior walls."

The manager wiped his hands on his paint-stained blue apron and walked over to the stacked cans. He bent to pick one up and, nodding between the can he held and some of the others stacked on the floor, he explained some of the differences. One brand held up to scuffs well, he said, and another was washable. One brand would require more coats than another.

"An inexpensive one is fine," the customer said. "It's just an apartment, so I'm not too worried about quality. I don't know how long I'll be there."

"Are you sure it's okay to paint?" the manager asked. He lowered the can back to its position on the stack. "A lot of places don't want you to paint when you're renting."

"It doesn't really matter," the customer said. He pointed to one of the cans. "Maybe I'll get this one. There's not much difference."

"That one's fine," the manager said. "How many gallons?"

"Two bedrooms and a living room. Small bedrooms. A big living room." The customer estimated the square feet of wall space out loud, talking his way through the math.

"You can probably do those rooms with a gallon each," the manager said. "The living room probably has more floor space, but not more wall space. People make that mistake a lot. If you run out, you can always come back." The manager grabbed three cans of paint—one in his left hand and two in his right—and carried them toward the back of the store. "Did you have some colors in mind?" he asked as he stepped behind the counter and back toward the mixer.

The customer drummed his fingers on the counter in a brief rhythm. "I'm looking for some muted colors," he said. "My son's three. He's excitable. He cries over candy bars and cereal boxes and whether or not his cartoons are on. That stage. I'm hoping maybe a light color in his room will help him keep his composure."

"Some people say they do that," said the manager.

The customer spread some color cards across the counter. "That's not a bad one," he said, pointing to a light square toward the end of a card with a series of greens. The square was labeled *Bok Choy*.

"For your son's room?"

"No," the customer said, "that one would be for the living room."

"The cards are set up so you can find other colors that might go with that one," the manager said. He showed the customer other cards from the same color family as the green, and the customer chose a blue and a lavender. The blue was called *Lovebird Feather*. The lavender was *Pastel Periwinkle*. "Those are good colors," the manager said. He removed the lid from one of the cans of paint, set the can under a machine next to the mixer, and entered a number on a keypad. Dye flowed from the machine into the paint. "My wife and I have a lavender like that in our bedroom," he said.

"It'll be for my girl's room," the customer said.

"It's a good color for a girl, too," the manager said. He used a rubber mallet to pound the lid back onto the dyed can of paint. He lowered the can into the mixer, closed the machine's lid, and pressed a button. The machine rattled to life with an oscillating roar that reminded the customer of a steam train. While the mixer ran, the customer walked through the store's short aisles, looking at supplies.

"So anyway, then there's another one," the younger employee said. He moved closer to the manager now that the customer had left the counter. "It's supposed to take place in the Ukraine, right? It's about this kid looking for his grandfather's old friends from back in the war, before his grandfather left to go to America. The friends saved his grandfather's life or something, but then his grandfather went to America and had a whole different life in America. So after the grandfather dies, the grandson goes back to see if he can find any of the old Ukraine people. But not a single part of it was made in the Ukraine. It was all made in Czechoslovakia."

"And you figured that one out, too?" said the manager. He dipped his finger into a can of mixed paint and then touched the finger to the lid, leaving a small oval of color.

"No, I read about that one in a magazine," said the younger employee. "There's no way to tell, because you can't tell what any of the signs say, because it's a different alphabet. You'd have to be from one of those places to know it was wrong."

The customer picked out a brown plastic roller handle,

some yellow roller covers, an aluminum tray, three black plastic tray liners, a paper dropcloth, and a small wooden paint brush. When the three cans were mixed, the customer returned to the counter and paid for the paint and supplies. The manager put some wooden stir sticks on the counter, too. "If you let these sit for any more than a day or two, you'll want to stir them up again," he said.

"That's fine," the customer said. "I'm going to try and do it all tonight. Do you have some plastic bags I could put these in?"

"We don't have bags," the manager said. "Do you want a box?"

"You don't have bags at all?"

"No bags."

"A box is fine."

The manager put the three cans of paint in one box and the other supplies in another. The customer put the box of supplies on top of the cans of paint and picked up the two boxes together. As he carried them toward the door, he walked past the younger employee, who was removing three cans of paint from a cart he had pushed to where all the different brands were stacked. The younger employee placed the cans in the vacant spots left where the manager had taken the cans of paint for the customer, and the row was complete and even again. The employee flipped the handles back to match the other handles. "You have a good night, now," he said, nodding to the customer as he passed.

The man stepped into the apartment, switched the light on with his elbow, and set the boxes down on the mottled brown-and-beige carpet. He pushed the boxes further into the room with his foot and then closed the door. In the room was a metal-framed futon sofa, a small end table with a lamp, an old television on a pressboard stand, and a bookshelf that held some hardback books, a small stereo, and some stacked papers and envelopes. The walls were light beige, and the trim along the floor and around the closet doors was the same beige, as were the walls of the kitchen and those of the short hallway that led back to the two bedrooms and the bathroom.

The man lifted the cans of paint from the box and set them in a line on the carpet. He emptied the box of supplies out onto the carpet, too, and then tore the plastic off one of the roller covers and pushed it onto the roller. He rolled it experimentally against his palm, and then went into the kitchen and started a pot of coffee. He took a roll of paper towels and a screwdriver from the kitchen counter, returned to the living room, and used the screwdriver to open the can of light green paint. He looked down into its thick, milky surface and then dipped his finger into the paint, lifted it out, and watched the paint run from the tip of his finger back into the can. He wiped his finger on a paper towel, turned on the stereo, and went into the kitchen to pour a cup of coffee. The radio announcer stumbled over the name of the song that had just played.

The man returned to the living room and spread the dropcloth along one of the walls. He poured some paint into the aluminum tray, rolled the roller back and forth until it was loaded with paint, and then rolled the paint onto the broad, empty wall.

After he'd covered only a few square feet, the telephone rang. The man set the roller in the tray and went to answer the phone where it sat on the carpet in the hallway.

He said hello and then he listened. "Painting," he said. "About what?" he said. "Randomly, for no reason?" he said. He paced up and down the short hallway. "That's completely screwed up, the same as always," he said. "This is all a repeat. It's sick," he said. "But that's how you feel about everyone," he said. "Exactly," he said. And he hung up the phone.

He walked counterclockwise around the living room, a rapid circle he completed three times. Then he went back to the paint tray and again took up the roller.

The work went quickly—the only places that required careful work with the small wooden brush were along the ceiling and around the trim that framed the front door and the closet door. When the man finished, he washed the wooden brush in the kitchen sink and threw the roller cover and plastic tray liner away. He put a clean plastic liner in the tray and filled his cup of coffee. He poured light blue paint into the tray and pushed a new roller cover onto the roller. In the first bedroom there was a low twin bed with a comforter covered in pictures of footballs and football helmets, basketballs and basketball hoops, and baseballs and baseball gloves. There was also a dark-stained pine nightstand with a small lamp, and a red toy box whose lid was attached with black metal hinges. The furniture had all been pushed into the center of the room. The man spread the dropcloth along one of the walls and began to paint.

Later, he washed the tray and wooden brush again, pushed a new brush onto the roller handle, and filled the tray with the lavender paint. The second bedroom had only a crib and a chest of drawers, again pushed to the center of the room. Again the man spread the dropcloth and began to paint. When he was finished, he washed all of the tools a last time and set them to dry on paper towels spread across the kitchen counter. He put the cans of paint in the closet and closed the door. After cleaning up, the man walked into the first bedroom and lay down on the twin bed. He turned off the lamp, pulled the comforter over himself, and went to sleep.

The man walked back into the paint store again a week later, carrying a can of paint. The manager with the close-cropped gray hair and glasses was again behind the counter, but this time he was working with a middle-aged woman who had long, thick blond hair and wide hips. The manager was wiping the counter with a rag. The woman was taking rolls of blue masking tape from a cardboard box and stacking them on a shelf.

"I need to buy another can of paint," the man said. "A different blue."

"Sure," the manager said. "You were here last week."

"It's for my son's room," the man said. He set his can of paint on the counter.

"He didn't like the one you chose?"

"He hasn't seen it," the man said. "I just think it's too dark. His room is pretty small, so maybe it's too much blue."

The manager looked at the lid of the can. He pulled some blue color cards from a drawer and set them on the counter. "Here's the one you have," he said, pointing to one of the squares. "A shade lighter is this one."

"That's fine," the man said.

The manager asked the woman to get him a fresh can of paint from the stack, and she walked across the store.

Nodding toward the can on the counter, the manager said, "I'm sorry, but I can't give you credit for this one. We don't do returns."

"I didn't expect you to," the man said.

"You also took a lavender, right?" the manager said.

The man nodded.

When the woman brought the fresh can of paint to the counter, the manager opened the lid and set the can under the dye machine. After the dye machine finished and the manager hammered the lid back onto the can, he lowered it into the mixer. The same oscillating roar filled the store, and the manager said, "He bought a lavender last week, like the one in our room. For a girl's room, right?"

The man nodded.

"It's a good color for any room," the woman said, smiling. "Did she like it?"

"She's ten months old," the man said. "So it doesn't really matter."

"A baby!" the woman said happily.

The manager lifted the can from the mixer and set it on the counter. "Anthony was talking about his movies again that night this gentleman was here," he said. "He talked for forty-five minutes almost without stopping."

"He pays attention to the strangest things," the woman told the man. "Like if a book on a table moves a little between shots, or if something about someone's clothes changes. They call it what?"

"Continuity errors," the manager said. "But now he's on to figuring out where they made the movies. If they use one place but call it another."

"I think trying to catch mistakes is the only reason he watches them," the woman said.

"Sometimes all his talking about drives me nuts and I

think I'm going to have to fire him," the manager said. "But then I get over it. Besides, if we fired him he'd just find someone else to go on about all his movies to. We might as well let him talk here so long as he's getting some work done."

"It's a community service," the woman said, and the two of them laughed.

The manager took the can of paint from the mixer and set it on the counter. He opened the lid, dipped his finger into the paint, and made an oval of color on the lid. He wiped his finger on a rag, hammered the lid back onto the can, rang up the price at the register, and took the customer's credit card. The customer signed the receipt and picked up his new can of paint.

"That's really a nice color," the woman said. "Hopefully your boy will like that one better. You wouldn't necessarily think it, but sometimes girls are easier to please. Boys can be picky, too."

"They haven't seen it," the man said. "Have you not been listening? I'm the only one that's seen it."

"I'm sorry," the woman said. "I didn't realize."

"Well I've said it more than once," the man said. "I've said it over and over."

The manager and the woman stood quietly as the customer left with his can of paint. They watched him walk along the sidewalk and past the front of the store.

It wasn't raining that night, and the car headlights that swept past along the street shone clean and clear through the windows. There was a gap in the row where the woman had pulled the can of paint for the customer. She went into the back room and came out with a can of paint.

Leviathan

It was really just a nice April evening when everything ended for me. The city had seen the sun that day for the first time in a month, so I had for the first time in a month walked along sidewalks that were dry and white rather than slick and dark, and for the first time in a month heard birdsong rather than rain. Juicy buds erupted from the trees' thin spring branches. The sky turned pink and orange behind the setting sun. The world was resurgent, filled with a sense of birth and possibility.

I was filled with dread. A trick was being played on me, I thought, or some kind of scam. I expected a movie tough—square-jawed, squinting, a real palooka—to step out of an alley, sock me in the gut, and take my wallet. Because something wasn't right. I couldn't tell what the something was, though: was the something *something*, or was the something me? I almost wanted the movie-tough scenario to be real, if only so that after the guy punched me, took my money, and walked away, I could slowly straighten myself and, in pain and maybe bleeding internally—why not?—I could at least know I'd been right.

But on that street, there were no alleys. Nor were there palookas, in that neighborhood or anywhere else in town. It was just me, walking. Alone.

I was headed to meet Ray Jennings. And I had never met with Ray Jennings before, but I knew who he was. Ray Jennings owned and operated the slickest magazines in town. Ray Jennings published *CityLife Portland*, the magazine that made Portland look like exactly the sleek and sophisticated city I believed it decidedly was not, and which annoyed me with that unhyphenated-but-internally-capped *CityLife* thing, a construction I felt had already become strained and dated long before *CityLife Portland* adopted it. By that point, the very idea of a word like *CityLife* struck me as so linguistically musty and mildewed as to seem almost Victorian. It was like naming a magazine *Uncle Arthur's List of Friendly Entertainments for Your Pleasant Week-End!* And Ray Jennings also published *Living Portland Style*, a magazine I had made fun of so many times I was exhausted by it—because how could you *live* a *style*? It didn't make sense, I'd already said to everyone I knew, It was like naming a magazine *Running Portland Shorts*, and besides, the people in *Living Portland Style* were dressed in a way that had absolutely nothing to do with the way anyone actually dressed in Portland, because no one in Portland dressed, Portland *had no style*, that was the whole point of Portland. And I could go on at length about that if anybody wanted, though no one did, least of all myself. And Ray Jennings published *Portland Culture Monthly*, which, I happened to have noticed, had recently shifted to a semi-monthly schedule. But they hadn't changed the name! And did that not say everything one needed to know about culture in Portland? That it was so culturally impoverished that even its cultural pretensions extended no further than the idea that its culture might be monthly, rather than semi-monthly? And then there were a few trashier things that had probably once been cash cows for Ray Jennings, like *Portland Singles Pages* and *Portland Music Pages* and *Portland Gallery Pages*, though those weaker little publications were almost completely dead by then, flipped from cash cows into pure losses once they were rendered redundant by social media sites and unemployed bloggers. That was what the name Ray Jennings represented to me. It represented wealth and the ways in which wealth lies to itself, it represented official culture and the ways in which official culture lies to itself, and it represented success and the ways in which success is contextual and undeserved and mostly a result of being a straight white male born in a certain year, having a certain kind of handshake, and possessed of a certain tone of voice. Some deep, reptilian structure in my brain—some core of neurons devoted only to dominance, violence, and hissing lizard battle—snapped immediately awake when I thought of Ray Jennings.

And yet there I was, sweating beneath my coat, gazing up at the buds that swelled like boils upon the trees, and gazing down at the slabs of sidewalk that passed one after another beneath my feet, as if I were traveling the path of the most boring and pointless board game ever invented. Except that the game ended at a restaurant where you had dinner with someone you hated.

I was a little raw that April. I was a little raw and a little touchy. I'd had a friend die in a stupid, pointless way a month earlier, and then I'd found out another friend was getting married. And I hate it when people get married, I've always hated it, because it's always the end—it's the same as the person dying. So I was losing people. Or I *felt* I was losing people.

Just a week before my dinner with Ray Jennings, I'd been sitting in a bar with my friend Luke—the one getting married—and with my fists on the table, I had leaned forward in the booth and, speaking about our friend Neil—the one who had died a stupid and pointless death—I had said, "And then I start to think that maybe I failed him as an *editor*. But Luke, what he pitched me was just so, so boring. I have to remind myself how boring his ideas were, because they were profoundly, maybe even *movingly* dead, dumb boring."

"He never mentioned anything to me. I didn't know he even pitched stuff to you," Luke said.

"Only all the time," I said. "Only all the fucking time."

We were in the Barley Mill, the place we used to drink when we were in grad school together. This was the first time I'd been back to the Barley Mill in years, though—I avoided the place like the plague. The lacquered wood, the Grateful Dead posters, the sloppy, hazed-out, jellybeard jam-band music always playing in the place: the Barley Mill was like returning to my childhood; it was like descending again into my parents' funky basement. But I was the one who had suggested we meet there, and who, upon stepping inside, immediately regretted it, because somehow I had forgotten about the skeletons. How had it not occurred to me that, wanting to talk about Neil, I had asked Luke to meet me in a bar filled with images of skeletons? I thought I had made a sentimental choice, because the place had been our hangout. But there sure were a lot of symbols of death in that place. And it was probably there inside the Barley Mill, beneath the slack-jawed skeletons grinning from their tie-dyed afterlife, that I started to slip into trouble.

"What were his story ideas?" Luke asked.

"Listen, he didn't even pay attention to what the magazines were about," I said. "He told me he wanted to write some kind of long, lyrical essay about a Thelonious Monk album, and what it meant to listen to it. He said he wanted to do it carefully, track by track, and I told him, Neil, the journal is about bicycling as an act of resistance. Do you know what he said? He said, 'But it's when I'm riding my bike that I listen to the Monk album. That would be part of the essay, how I listen to it on my bike.' And I'm sitting there thinking, *Neil, you stupid fucking son of a bitch. No one is interested in your super in-depth essay about an old Thelonious Monk album.* And you know how I am."

"Maybe," Luke said.

"You know how I am," I said. "Here's how I am: I can immediately think of at least thirty reasons I will never, ever, under any circumstance, run Neil's in-depth essay on getting moony over Monk while riding over the fucking Hawthorne Bridge while musing upon the waters below. I can give reasons that have to do with the journal he wants me to put this thing in, I can give reasons that have to do with what people want to read in general, and I can get theoretical on his ass and talk about how corporate Middle America swallowed classic jazz whole and spat it back out as decorative music for Starbucks. It has been completely and entirely evacuated of any meaning whatsoever, both Walter Benjamin and Miles Davis understood this perfectly well—that was the whole point of Miles Davis going bat-shit crazy, and for Neil to not be aware of this is a mark against him as a thinker at any number of very real and greatly concerning levels. Can you picture that? The hell I was going through while I listened to him give me these story ideas?"

"I think so," Luke said. "Mostly because you're yelling it at me this very minute."

"I'm not yelling," I said. But I probably was. Because the place had too much weight. I kept thinking that my mother was somewhere in The Barley Mill, smoking Virginia Slims and about to yell at me after stepping on another one of my Legos. And I kept feeling like Neil—who had been riding his bike home from a bar one night when he was hit and killed by a car whose driver had not stopped, had not been caught, and who was *still out there somewhere*—was going to stumble around the corner any second, sweaty and out of breath from having busted there as fast as he could on his bike, but still maintaining that nervous smile of his, as if he were constantly abashed about some little faux pas he had committed, though he had never actually committed any that I knew of, other than dying in a stupid fucking unnecessary way. I expected him to flop down in the booth with that uncertain look on his face and then, when we stared at him in wordless amazement, to look back at us and say something like, "What?" The desperate grip the Barley Mill's owners and regulars held on their eternal Jerry Garcia moment—it was too earnest, too *real*. And to think that Luke and Neil and I had sat in there on any number of occasions during grad school, arguing the pointless while getting drunk on Pabst. That had been a lifetime ago. And I had used exactly none of that knowledge in the seven years since grad school, the years during which I had managed or edited or published the five little journals or magazines or whatever the hell it was I was publishing. If someone had come to me when I was in the thick of poring over Foucault and Derrida and Foucault and Butler and Foucault and Lacan, highlighter in hand and just endlessly entertaining myself—and boring everyone who came within twenty yards of me—with my theories about theory and my theories about my theories about theory, if someone had come to me and said, Look, none of this matters, because during the next seven years you will become the publisher of *Spoke! The Journal of Bicycle-as-Resistance*, and of *Purl Grrrl, Where Urban Knitters Unite*, and of *Never Run: Diary of a Bus Hound*, and of *Outdoor Shag: Green Options for the Urban Do-It-Yourselfer*, and finally of *Portland Underground: Almanac of the City Undiscovered*, if someone had come to me and said, Put down the Foucault, friend, and back away, because you'll be going into the stupidest business there is, I would have denied it. I would have told this messenger from the future that he was dead wrong, that yes, I complained often about print media, about the way false authority was used to peddle false status, about haute mimesis run haute amok in the city's glossy pages, but that was because I wanted nothing to do with it. I would have responded by quoting Foucault. That's what I would have done.

But there I was, slumped back into the booth, because yes, maybe Luke was right, maybe I had been yelling. So in what I thought was a carefully normal voice I said, "But that's the kind of shit he was coming to me with. Can he write in the urban knitting magazine about being a nonknitter? No, I said, I'm not the editor of these things, I just publish them. And the actual editor of the magazine isn't going to have it, even if you *are* my friend, Neil."

"He never mentioned any of this to me," Luke said.

"Never?"

"Not once."

I hadn't seen Luke in over six months, but the guy seemed exactly the same. He was still the tall, thin, loping guy that on first sight makes you think, So this dude is either an artist, fronts a band, or kills, serially, on the weekends. It was his long lashes, his sad eyes—the sheer *heavy-liddedness* of him. He was on some private metaphysical journey, it seemed, a trek purely instinctual, almost animal, which betrayed its presence only through the impression he gave of carrying some invisible leviathan burden, but comfortably. It was the source of the tragic, brilliant, but ultimately withheld utterance that he seemed always on the verge of. Jesus, I thought, this guy could probably have any woman in this room with that look.

But what had he done? What had he really done? Nothing. Seven years ago he'd said he was going to make an independent film, and he noodled around on a screenplay, and then got an office job reconciling accounts of some kind for a health care company I never bothered to remember the name of. And now he was going to marry his girlfriend, and they were probably going to buy a house and have a baby and watch television for the rest of their lives. Those looks, that bearing, his deep and abiding intelligence? He had done nothing. I sat there in the Barley Mill, one week before I would sit down with Ray Jennings, and thought: We have, all of us, done nothing.

And then Ray Jennings took twenty minutes to get around to saying why he had asked to meet with me. And during those twenty minutes of introducing ourselves and chatting, of trading small talk about the restaurant, and what restaurant that restaurant had been before, and what restaurant it had been before that; of sharing memories of what the neighborhood had been like during the tenure of each of those restaurants, and which of those restaurants we had eaten at; of discussing the weather, and mutually appreciating the clear sky and agreeing that its presence was a relief, an incredible relief; and of exchanging any number of the little conversational touches, reassurances, and tonal strokes that two people who have never spoken before but are sitting down in a little restaurant to try to get to know one another usually exchange, I had been doing my best to answer nothing but the question *Why has this man asked me here?* Yes, I occasionally bought his magazines. Who didn't? They were *the magazines*. They showed you how the elites decorated their fancy lofts, what kinds of dogs they were forcing into coitus to make their designer puppies, who was running the show, and what kinds of false compliments people were paying in print to the people running the show. All of this was useful, and yes, I kept track, and probably a little more closely than most. Okay: probably a lot more closely. But that didn't explain why Ray Jennings had e-mailed me a couple days before, why he'd introduced himself in the e-mail as if I might not know who he was, and why in the e-mail he had then complimented me on the first issue of *Portland Underground: Almanac of a City Undiscovered* before saying he'd like to meet me, and would I want to get together after work some day, maybe at Le Happy?

It didn't make any sense. *Portland Underground* was not a kick-ass publication. The three guys putting *Portland*

Underground together were cool, thrashing-around-town dudes, but actually laying out and prepping the pages of that first issue of *Portland Underground*, I had definitely thought, Yep, bike polo, tall bikes, klowns with a *k*, art walks, poetry slams, yep—none of this is underground. There is nothing in even this first issue of *Portland Underground* that is at all underground. But of course I printed the thing anyway, and sold two hundred copies within two weeks, and then printed two hundred more and sold those. And that was four hundred bucks in my pocket, because that's how I was doing it in those days. And don't ever, ever do that, by the way. Don't ever say, You know what, I'm going to make little magazines or journals or what have you, about little topics I'm interested in or not interested in, and then I'll sell them and rely on those sales to live and buy food. It's a stupid idea.

So I just did a very good job of being engaging and honest and witty in my discussion of *Portland Underground* and *Purl Grrl* and all the others during those first twenty minutes of dinner, of just being Mr. Friendly Pants, all while thinking: Is this guy threatened by me? Is he trying to steal story ideas? Is he plumbing me for the supposed zeitgeist? Am I going to say something in this conversation that will show up in *Portland Culture Monthly* next month? Or two months from now, as it were. Hah. What's going on? Is he gay? Does he know I'm gay? No. There's no way. If Ray Jennings were gay, I would already know. But maybe he's one of these older, closeted, entirely repressed types, the kind who waits until his kids go off to college before being so bold as to indulge himself by having a drink with a young man. Was this *that*?

I looked at the guy. The guy was chinos and a collared

long-sleeved merino sweater. He was a close shave and a regular haircut and a wedding ring and confidence. This wasn't that. So my mind continued to spin: speaking, watching, recording. What Ray just said, what I just said, play it back but freeze that word—why *that* tone, why *that* response, was that a business response or a personal response, is *he* leading the conversation or am I? He went to college *where*—remember that, look it up later—and I am saying *what*? Why am I saying that, stop saying that. Ask him about his printer, ask about his print runs. No, just ask about his printer.

What was this?

And then Ray Jennings finally said, "Well, I'm sure you're wondering why I wanted to meet with you."

And I said, "I'll admit it, yes. I am absolutely wondering that."

And he sighed and looked at me with the narrowed eyes of friendly appraisal, or maybe of *faux*-friendly appraisal, and then as if it were as routine a task as deciding on a new pair of shoes, he said, "I'm looking for a managing editor for *Portland Culture Monthly*. And I have some internal people who want the job, but I don't know. I'm starting to worry we're just reproducing the same thing over and over. That's what magazines are, of course, but *PCM*, as you know, has had to slip back to publishing every other month."

"Really?" I said. "I hadn't noticed."

"Yes," Ray Jennings said, "So it's in transition, in terms of what it is and what it could be, which makes me nervous about hiring internally. I think we need new blood, or a new attitude, because if the thing has nothing to offer anyone, if it slips out of touch, then we lose it. I'm not yet convinced that a print magazine doesn't have a place. It has a place. But I'm fifty-two years old, and I suspect I should ask for some help deciding what a print magazine is in the twenty-first century."

"Are you saying this has been an interview?" I asked. "Without me knowing it?"

He laughed. "No, I wouldn't do that to you. But also: yes, kind of. Because I just picked up on the fact that you're running all of these little things, which seems exhausting to me, and kind of impossible, frankly. I don't know how you manage your time or coordinate all of these things, and it occurred to me that you would have to have all sorts of different skills in order to be doing all of this stuff—if you are, in fact, actually doing all of it yourself. So I thought I should meet you."

"Right," I said. And my mind had stopped spinning. But now it didn't seem to be moving at all.

"And I don't hire people myself," Ray Jennings said. "Actually hiring someone involves a formal interview with me and two associate editors, and it takes place in the office, and then I talk it over with those editors. But it's not a conversation of equals, because I'm the publisher and it's my money, so my opinion counts for more than theirs. So I guess what I'm saying is that I'd like to spend the rest of dinner here talking about the possibility of you formally applying for the position of managing editor at *Portland Culture Monthly*."

I thought, This is a setup. I said, "But this isn't an interview."

"No," he said. "Because I don't know you at all, and I don't know what your goals are, and I don't know what your background is. This is a dinner between two publishers. I publish things in Portland, and so do you, so I wanted to meet you. That's what this is. But I think the topic of our publishers-getting-to-know-one-another dinner might naturally include what's going on in Portland publications these days, and what kind of positions might be open in Portland publishing these days."

"And specifically, what kind of position is open at *your* publication."

"Sure. If you want to talk about that. Or about what that position would entail."

I looked around the room. Le Happy wasn't a big place—it was red walls, white tablecloths, and a little bar in the back corner where the sole waitress went to gossip with the bartender when she wasn't attending to the diners. There were maybe eight tables, all of them filled with strangers. The sun had gone down. We were all dining together, by candlelight.

"But we don't have to," Ray Jennings said. "We could just have dinner."

Right. Because that very afternoon, I had just been having lunch in a vegan bakery with the editor of *Purl Grrrl*, and she had just been telling me about any number of stories she had lined up for her fifth issue. Part three of four in her "Knitted Closet" series—this time it was a belt. Her idea that someone could knit herself an entire outfit had struck me as simultaneously obvious and ridiculous, but part one had been a peasant blouse, and part two, pants. Actually wearing, at the same time, each of the four knitted garments in this four-part series would announce you as a total idiot, and yet I hadn't said this, I'd just sat there, listening to Purl Grrrl go on about what was slated for the issue. Knitting and the environment. The economics of knitting. Knitting vis-à-vis the concept of "slow clothing." Knitting history. A think piece on macramé. And I had nodded to it all while looking at the woman, who had white-girl dreadlocks and a multiply-pierced face, and who leaned enthusiastically forward, practically spitting crumbs of her muffin at me as she explained how totally killer the next issue of *Purl Grrl* was going to be. All I could think was: I'm sitting here in Banana Republic slacks and a J. Crew sweater, and I'm wearing Alain Mikli glasses frames. I dress this way—and I maintain decent posture, use a high-quality pen on a standard yellow legal pad, and finish swallowing before I start speaking—specifically in order to differentiate myself from the mussed-hair hipster vibe that has swallowed this town whole, because 95 percent of the time, the people rocking that vibe have adopted it with sheeplike docility. And I don't care about knitting, I'm not up nights over the environment, and I eat meat. Am I not everything this woman claims she is against? And yet I'm listening to her talk about *Purl Grrrl*, and she is, at length, telling me about it. Why? Why am I here? Why am I doing this? And then I thought: Right. Because I am a moron. Let's be plain, I thought: If I were as smart as I think I am, I wouldn't be sitting in a vegan bakery, signing off on *Purl Grrrl* so that I can get the issue out on time, so that between that and the other publications I keep restocking at the handful of bookstores still in business in town, I might make enough money to barely pay for one more month of my bare-bones life. And it is not the life of a genius. There comes a time when we must admit that an objective observer would not find this life the work of a genius.

These same thoughts were sending my foot into anxious

tapping there beneath the table as I sat across from Ray Jennings: *tap tap tap tap tap*. And not only that, but some of the tapping was a result of the fact that I was beginning to *like* Ray Jennings. I did not want to like him. I thought this person's publications were bullshit, quite frankly. I thought *Portland Culture Monthly* was trash for rich white people and pretentious liars, and that, *quite frankly*, there was a lot of crossover in those demographics. I thought I would rather try in vain to find things that actually *were* underground, and fail, than lie to myself month after semi-month about how amazing the Impressionist stuff was going to be at the art museum, for instance, or about what a daring choice the ballet had made in its staging of *The Nutcracker* that winter. I sat there looking at Ray Jennings and thought: *I don't want to lie to myself.* And what I said to him was: "I don't want to lie to you."

"I don't want you to lie to me, either," he said.

"Because I need to admit to some disdain, and to some problems I have with your publications."

"Disdain is fine," he said. "I was worried it might be outright contempt. I was prepared for you to never even answer my e-mail."

"Right," I said, while at the same time thinking: *Huh?* "And also, you've called me here under false pretenses. You're asking me to talk to you about your magazine, but how do I know you won't listen to what I say here tonight and then just go back and implement some changes yourself, and never pay me a dime for my thoughts?"

"You *don't* know that," he said, as if it were obvious. "All I can say is that's not my intention."

"So I have to trust you? When I don't know you at all?"

"What would you like? As a show of good faith."

"I ordered a beer," I said. "But that's not what I wanted."

"What do you want?"

"Vodka. Some good, maybe even expensive, vodka."

He smiled and beckoned the waitress. When she came over he said, "We'd like to have some vodka. Grey Goose for me, on the rocks. And you?"

"Grey Goose sounds fine," I said.

"Two, then," he told her. And when the waitress left, he said, "Is that sufficient? As a show of good faith?"

"It's a start," I said.

"So we can talk about *Portland Culture Monthly*?"

"Semi-monthly, actually."

"Okay," he said, smiling as if I were perfectly charming. "*Portland Culture* Semi-*Monthly*."

But listen: in that moment, I felt like I no longer had any thoughts about that at all. Because I was on the verge of running out the door. And the reason was that Ray Jennings was speaking to me as if I were a real person. Ray Jennings was so diabolical, he understood that if he acted as if I were an actual person, a man who merited being spoken to as if everything I had been doing with those little magazines was actually real, then he could lock me into being that person. By which I mean the person I already was. I had been dressing business bourgeois for some time. I had been developing analytical thoughts on magazines and how they worked and what they should be for even longer. It didn't start that evening—it was just the first time someone had actually asked. And it was motherfucking evil genius Ray Jennings who was asking, because he was going to turn me into the person I already was.

Did he not understand that the entire thing was a bluff? Was it not totally obvious to him that what my father had said more than once was true, that my entire life was an ornate game with all kinds of crazy rules whose sole purpose was for me to never, ever have to have a job? And that it was a game so stupid that the reward for winning was *nothing*? I believe Ray Jennings understood *all* of this. I believe he sensed it within only a few minutes of sitting down with me, and that by the time he ordered that vodka, he knew exactly what he was doing.

And I was falling for *everyone* that spring, anyway. When I'd been sitting across from Luke in the Barley Mill, I couldn't stop thinking about how much I liked the guy, how he was the perfect person to talk to, how I could insult him up and down for an hour and he would just be amused. How he was *untouchable*. You could throw every kind of childish fit of anger at Luke, and he'd just give you that little verbal pat: *I know*. The wry little sideways smile. He was a profound being, patrolling the depths, I thought. You never saw him and he never said anything, and then you called him up and said, Look, I need to talk about Neil, and I know you're getting married pretty soon, so can we please get a drink somewhere before you disappear forever into stupid middle class banality? And his response was just, *Sure*. And when you showed up, there he was, unmarked, unchanged, doing nothing and having done nothing. The deep cetacean *brood* of the guy, I thought. It was like he lived secretly informed by some wordless baleen conspiracy, his soul a creature that just eyed you sidewise as it cruised past and then disappeared into the ink-black distance while you rolled in its wake. I actually *thought* that. I constructed that sentence and enunciated it aloud in my head. I was in a very raw and vulnerable place.

"Are you seeing anyone?" he asked me in the Barley Mill.

"What? No. Why?"

"Because that's your third vodka, and you always drink vodka when you're not seeing anyone."

"That's not true. I'm drinking because of Neil." I was bouncing my leg there, too, but I couldn't stop it. I put my own hands on my own leg to try and stop it from bouncing, and the leg kept bouncing. Basketball highlights rolled past on the television in the corner. Drunk college kids failed to shoot pool with any kind of facility. A joke, I thought, they're a joke, we're all a joke. "What happened to Neil is fucked up," I said. "And I think it's fucking *me* up."

"I know," Luke said.

"I need to smoke a cigarette," I said. "Why can't you smoke a cigarette anywhere anymore?"

So we stepped out to the street, and after I'd taken a couple deep drags—after the nicotine had hit my blood and begun to do its work—Luke asked for a cigarette, too.

"What are you talking about?" I said. "You smoke now? Why are you smoking?"

"I'm smoking because it makes you feel better," he said.

Don't cry, I thought. Don't cry. Just tap your foot and smoke. Look around. You're just outside. You're just smoking a cigarette.

"It's going to be okay," he said.

"No," I said. "No, Neil's dead, and someone out there killed him, and I don't understand it."

"Don't talk," he said. "Just smoke."

But the words kept tumbling out. "I think maybe I should have run one of those stories he said he wanted to write. Why don't I have a magazine where people can write super boring but probably brilliant and original stuff about Thelonious Monk?"

"Because nobody does that," Luke said. "And it's not your job to do it."

"I know. I know." I wanted Luke to hug me. I wanted him to just hold me very, very tightly. "You should write something for me," I said. "Why don't you ever write something for me?"

"I don't think I have anything to say."

"Just make something up. Write something about urban knitting. On the bus. These people I'm working with are freaks and they can't spell their own names. Just write something about anything. Write something about Thelonious Monk. Please write something about Thelonious Monk."

"You're a mess," he said.

"I am not," I said. "You're the mess."

"You've lost control of yourself," he said.

And then I said a lot of things. I told Luke he was a failure, that he'd never done anything, and that was why he had nothing to say and was going to get married now, so he could go off and be dead in front of a television set. I told him he was probably going to have a bunch of kids and never do anything interesting again, ever, and it was all over. He had never achieved anything, because he had never tried, and it was a fucking shame—it was a fucking shame that the slacker aesthetic had grabbed him by the throat and thrown him to the ground and ordered him never, ever to do anything, to just lie there and be still. Neil was dead, Luke was a failure, and I was the only one still trying, I said. And after I'd finished saying all of that stuff—after I had trusted him with my insanity, after I had laid myself bare before him like that—he had just looked at me and said, "Trying to do *what?*"

I never even tried to answer him. Because how could

he ask me that? I didn't say another thing to him. I just turned and walked away. I crossed the street, and went down another, and kept going. I walked away.

So all that stuff was in there when I started talking to Ray Jennings. And I should not have had the vodka he ordered, and I should not have started believing in the idea of me that he was selling to me, because it was too close to the one I had been selling to myself. And I certainly bought it. Because when Ray Jennings said, "I want you to come by the office tomorrow. I want to keep throwing these ideas around, and I want us to start thinking about what would make this work for you," what I replied was: "Okay." And then afterward—after Ray Jennings had shaken my hand, slipped into his spotless Acura, and driven off to his designer home in the West Hills, with his living room view of the city below and Mount Hood beyond—I had started walking home. And Ray Jennings was fine. Ray Jennings had just made a good decision.

It was dark. But it was still warm, still spring, and in the glow of the pale green streetlight that buzzed overhead, I could still see the juicy buds on the trees. They were chartreuse in the light—veined, serrated, and crisply psychedelic—and the sidewalk before me seemed a fuzzed but radiant gray, as if it had just been laid down. Off in the shadows, I heard something move—an animal, probably, shuffling toward cover. And I started chanting something, at first in my head, without realizing it, but then in a whisper that I heard myself say. And I kept on chanting it, in almost a speaking voice, as I walked away from the meeting at which I'd earned my first real job ever. "It's over," I was repeating in time with each of my strides. "It's over, it's over, it's over."

The Spiral

Michael stood at the window and looked down, surprised to discover that his fourteenth-floor room offered an unobstructed view of the library. He hadn't planned that, and it was odd to realize, when he pulled back the curtain, that his first glimpse would be from this overhead angle. He could see the exterior familiar to him from photos: the steel beams intersecting in a diamond pattern, the glass curtain walls that canted at odd angles as the building rose. It looked like a stack of old books that had been stepped on, he thought, the covers and bindings twisting beneath the pressure of the foot. One critic had described it as a partially crushed aluminum can. Another had just written, *I trust we'll run a photo.* In the gloom of the rainy afternoon, the building's transparent exoskeleton left the interior floors easily visible—like nicely stacked blocks within a shiny mesh gift bag, he thought. His mind continued casting about for further metaphors until he reminded himself that wasn't necessary.

Beyond downtown, a cloud of mist hung over the bay. The mile between the hotel and the shore was a steady descent, each street lower than the next, and this, combined with the height of his room, created an optical illusion in which the bay appeared to rise toward the horizon like a long gray hill, all of that water suspended, in defiance of gravity, upon an impossible slope. He studied the dark buildings, the shifting slabs of cloud, and the water gone milk gray in the wind and rain. A movie was playing on the television behind him while he watched a long black tanker plow through the bay, close to disappearing behind the dark glass side of a skyscraper that rose from Fourth Street. HANJIN, the white letters on the side of the tanker read. *He's that way*, an actress was saying, *He's always been that way.* The tanker began to pass behind the building. HAN, it soon read.

What did he say to you? the actress asked.

HA

He did? I can't believe that. He's a liar.

H

But I still miss him. I wish he was here.

The last section of the boat disappeared into the building as if diving into an ocean of black glass.

What are you looking at? the actress said.

"Nothing," Michael said. "The bay."

"Mr. Novak?" the woman said as she stepped from behind the counter. "My name is Sofie. I've been expecting you."

She stood in front of him, making no move to shake his hand. A web of pale veins was visible beneath the skin at her temple, where her hair was pulled back in loose braids.

Dark circles shone beneath her eyes, and her lack of expression made Michael suspect she wasn't thrilled with her assignment.

"I'm sorry to bother you," he said. "I'd just like the perspective of someone who works here, who has lived in the building and understands it. I'm sure I would overlook things if I just walked around alone."

"It's no problem. I give tours because I like to. Should we start here in children's?" She walked ahead of him, but with her head canted in his direction, as if apologizing for the necessity of leading. They passed over a highly-polished wood floor from which carved letters rose in nonsensical configurations, some backwards, some upside down, not all of them English. He studied the string passing beneath his feet: STV ΛΓKILO OMAOX, it read. Then the letters stopped and the floor became smooth, reflecting the hundreds of light fixtures shaped like oversized bulbs that hung from the exposed concrete ceiling. In the children's room, Sofie showed him the computers and the magenta foam chairs and the bulging purple discs of hard foam that could serve as either tables or additional seats. A purple wall behind the information desk and a bright yellow wall at the back of the room, the colors so deeply saturated and highly lit that they glowed, were the lone instances of color within the otherwise sober gray of the concrete pillars and ceiling. They left the children's room and crossed back to the other side of the lettered floor—NΛMU ΛIRΛMX, he read this time—where she led him into the auditorium. Lime green plastic seats stretched across the room in long, curving rows. He brushed his palm against the undulating folds of a twenty-foot-high curtain that covered the long wall behind the lectern.

"The curtain was designed by Petra Blaisse," Sofie said. "She's Koolhaas's girlfriend, I guess."

"I thought he was married." The curtain's pattern of hazy greens and browns called to mind a blurred image of a forest.

"He is, I think. Or was. Probably still is." She laughed. "I'm sorry. I don't know. I don't keep up on his personal life."

"But you're a fan of architecture?"

"Oh, I don't know. I know I like this building. I went to some of the meetings back when they were planning it. It seemed like it was going to be the most important place in town."

"Did you meet him?"

"Koolhaas? Once. But we didn't chat or anything. I just shook his hand and said something stupid."

Michael couldn't tell how old this young library tour guide was. Any answer between twenty-three and thirty-five seemed equally possible. "What did you say?"

"I said, 'I'm Dutch, and I'm proud to have a building designed by you here in my city.'"

"*Sofie* is Dutch? I thought it was Italian."

"It's the Dutch version of a common name. Mine is S-O-F-I-E."

Something about her willingness to spell the difference charmed him—the desire to be known correctly, maybe. "How old are you?" he asked.

"Why?"

"Because I can't tell."

"Men aren't supposed to ask a woman's age."

"I know."

"So I don't have to answer," she said, smiling. "So the answer is no answer."

"Fair enough," he said. "And I don't think it was a stupid thing to say."

The escalators to the next level had bright yellow frames that, within the gray concrete walls and low concrete ceiling of the channel they were rising through, practically glowed. Sofie stood sideways, two steps above Michael. She wore a slightly pilled blue v-neck sweater and dark blue jeans over black boots. Earrings with small blue and green beads dangled past her earlobes. "Are you writing about the building?" she asked, studying her boots.

Michael was wearing a charcoal gray suit, immaculately polished black shoes, and chunky, trapezoidal glasses whose frames had been handcrafted by a small French company. He had seen no one else in the library wearing a suit, and looking at Sofie's frayed jeans and scuffed boots, he realized that the way he was dressed seemed an affectation. Or was one. "No," he said. "It's years too late for that."

"I liked your article on the Trade Center."

"What article on the Trade Center?"

"From the *Rocky Mountain News*. It was a few years ago."

"More than just a few years ago. I thought you said the only building you were interested in was this one."

"But of course I look up the people they tell me I'm giving tours to. And your newspaper puts its stories online."

"Not anymore, they don't. They're out of business. And I don't think they're supposed to have old stuff online, either."

"It might have been posted on some other site."

"What site?"

"I don't know. I was using Google. I don't remember."

"Sofie, how long do you spend researching the people you give tours to?"

She laughed. "Don't worry—not very long. So if that newspaper is out of business, what are you doing now?"

"Right now? I'm looking at this library."

"For another newspaper?"

"Women are not supposed to ask a man about his employment status."

"That's not true. That's not a rule."

"No. I'm not working for another newspaper."

They stepped from the escalator into a shower of light. Michael looked up and saw, from inside now, the glass walls rising overhead. They allowed unobstructed views of the traffic on the street, and of the glass sides of the office buildings across the street whose innumerable windows reflected images of the library back at itself. Inside, the floors above the level Michael was currently on occupied less space—people stood at balconies at higher and higher levels, looking down to the main lobby, where Michael and Sofie now stood. A fifty-foot concrete wall rose through the middle of the building, and throngs of people wandered past, gazing up at the wall and at the floors overhead, or down at the immense floral pattern on the carpet that stretched across a large section of the floor. It's a cathedral, he thought, with wire mesh instead of stained glass. There were no icons, but the impression of a presence looking down remained. *Here's the church, here's the steeple*, a childish voice sang in his head. He felt his throat tighten and his pulse rise as he scanned the crowd, unsure if it was the sudden presence of all these faces at different levels that was causing the response, or if it was just that saying aloud that he was unemployed had triggered every feeling he was trying to ignore today. "I feel like I'm in the atrium of a five-star hotel," he said, though that wasn't what he felt, and he was aware of the comment's banality.

"This is the Living Room," Sofie said. "There's obviously seating here, as well as the main information desk, where I usually work. And there's a gift shop and a coffee cart there, next to where new fiction is shelved."

"Coffee, gifts, and fiction. This is the building's strip mall."

"It's just a small gift shop. Nothing gaudy."

His eyes were scanning the room, but without taking in any information. It took a conscious effort for him to focus on Sofie, and though he was aware he'd just said something possibly insulting, he couldn't recall exactly what it was.

"Are you alright?" she said.

"I'm fine," he heard himself say. "I just need a cup of coffee. Can I get you one?"

"No, thank you. Did you want a few minutes to sit down? Or were you—"

"Maybe. Yes, maybe."

"I could come back in five minutes. Or if you need longer, I can—"

"No, that sounds good. Five minutes. Thank you."

There had been moments in his life when he'd had the sense of watching himself from outside of his body, but what he was feeling now—and more and more often lately—was the opposite: he had tumbled down into some space from which he could only barely see other people, and had little sense of what they could see or hear of him. He could communicate in simple shorthand only, it seemed. *I need a cup of coffee. I will see you here in five minutes. I am really a normal person.*

While he stood in line for coffee, he watched Sofie slip behind a long, marble desk and stand next to a man with wavy brown and gray hair and sad, deep-set eyes. She smiled at something the man said, and when she said something back, he smiled, too, and looked toward the coffee cart. Michael looked quickly away, wondering if they were talking about him, and if so, what they were saying. To be spoken about in a way that produced smiles annoyed him. When he got his coffee, he took a seat in one of the large, modern chairs—these, too, were of molded foam—and studied the high concrete wall as he tried to compose himself. A middle-aged man in a business suit stood nearby, talking on a cell phone. "I'm in it right now," he was saying. "It's bizarre. It makes no sense. It's just bullshit. He probably laughed all the way back to Denmark, or wherever the hell he's from."

Michael stared at the patch of carpet between his feet as he imagined beating the man: the way his right fist would hit the man's cheekbone, followed by a left to the stomach that would double him over, and then a right uppercut that would finish him off, leaving the man on the floor with blood running from his mouth. You are just angry that this man has a job and money, he told himself. And speaks stupidly. You are angry because you believe stupid men shouldn't have things. You are nonsense.

He tapped his foot rapidly against the carpet. Rather than helping, the coffee was making him nauseous. He knew the entire causal chain of his condition. The nausea was the result of anxiety, the anxiety was the result of stress in his life, and the stress in his life was the result of, in no particular order, his protracted unemployment; the ongoing break-up of his marriage; the protracted custody battle he was having with the woman he had once loved; and the mountain of debt all of that added to. Which of those last things were causes and which were effects was a topic of dispute by various parties. Michael knew that what he needed to do was just breathe, though breathing, of course, could also be seen as the root problem—breathing, eating, walking, talking, racking up lawyer's bills while not actually having any money, borrowing money from his parents and brother in order to pay the rent on his little one-bedroom apartment and to buy groceries for himself and his four-year-old son on the two nights a week his wife allowed him to spend with the boy. The credit card and family debt he was building up had become unseemly and embarrassing. If he couldn't find a job, he would go bankrupt. If he went bankrupt, he would not be granted custody of his child. If he could not pay child support, he would what? End up in jail? Shoot himself in the head? Breathing was not going to make any of this go away.

"Ready to move on?" Sofie was standing next to him, her face an expression of innocent inquiry that changed to concern when he looked up. "Is everything okay? I can come back later."

"No, I was just thinking about something." He stood, carefully placing his feet shoulder-width apart in an attempt to seem relaxed. "Tell me about the wall. Curtains, lettered floors, lights, escalators, concrete monoliths—it's theater."

"But very much a working library," she said. "It's a working library *first*."

"With a fifty-foot concrete wall on which the search terms people are typing into the library's computers are supposed to be projected in some huge stream of words and numbers." He wondered if they were arguing now. He couldn't seem to manage his voice or tone.

"That part didn't happen, because of confidentiality. And yes, at first a lot of people thought this would just be a tourist attraction. I'm just a media assistant—not a real librarian—and I thought it would be hard to get transferred here, but it turned out to be easy, actually. Most of the librarians just want to work in a quiet place, and a lot of them think it's too busy here. But I find it relaxing—though in an energizing way. I guess I find places like this kind of spiritual."

"There are other places like this?"

She laughed. "I guess not. I just mean things like ocean views, or restaurants at sunset with a glass of wine in front of you. There's a restaurant called Place Pigalle down by the market, and it has a view of the bay and the ferries, and the ocean out beyond. Sometimes I go there straight from work, and the mood seems unbroken. That's all I mean. Should we go up to the Mixing Room?"

He nodded, but when he stepped forward, his legs felt weak. His hands were shaking and his face felt hot. *I shouldn't be here*, he thought. They were nearly to the escalator that would carry them to the next level, but something had gone wrong with his balance. He felt as if he were on the deck of a boat tilting in the sea, and when he tried to step in the direction of the escalator, the result was off by a significant degree. "Sofie," he said, and she turned back to him, startled.

He lay on the bed and stared at the daylight bleeding past the edges of the curtain, trying to recall Sofie's expression when he had begun stepping sideways while telling her he was ill. His peripheral vision had gone dark, and he had just managed to make it to the wall without falling. He had steadied himself—palm against concrete, breathing deeply—while his balance and vision returned. Had she been concerned for him, or just confused? Had she told him a time that she, personally, could lead him on a tour the next day, or had she just given him a time that somebody else could? He couldn't remember, and then, the next thing he knew, he was waking up there on the bed. He understood he was in a hotel room, and his watch told him it was four o'clock in the afternoon, but it took him several seconds to remember he was in Seattle, Washington, a fact he only felt fully certain about when he pulled back the room's curtain and found the library there, just as it had been that morning. Taking a seat at the room's little desk, he opened his laptop and checked his e-mail, but there was only one message—from his wife. *Could you come over this evening and help me move some stuff?* it read. *I want to sell some things.*

He typed: *I'm not in town. I'm in Seattle, working on a piece for Lucas. I'll be back Friday in time to pick up James from daycare.*

He sent it. Lucas was his former editor at the *Rocky Mountain News*. When the paper had gone under, Lucas had gotten an editorial position at *Situate*, an architecture and design magazine headquartered in Manhattan. Michael had heard through the grapevine—from a Boston architect Michael had interviewed for a freelance piece after the *Rocky* folded—that the Editor in Chief at *Situate* had possibly contacted Lucas to see if it was okay to talk to *Michael*. If true, this message had never been relayed. If true. Lucas had gotten Michael his job at the *Rocky* in the first place, and he'd run two different pieces from Michael in *Situate* in that first year after the *Rocky* folded, both of which paid well. So it was hard to say. But it was also true that when the paper went under, Lucas and his wife and two kids, both in junior high school, moved to Manhattan, where Lucas had gotten a job with *Situate*. And Michael did not move anywhere.

"Hello, Michael Novak," Lucas said when answering his phone.

"Hi, Lucas. I hope I'm not interrupting your dinner."

"It's okay, we're between courses. What's up?"

"I'm in Seattle, looking at the library here, and I was wondering if you'd have any interest in a piece on it."

There was a brief rustling on the line. Lucas was re-situating himself, or maybe walking further from whomever he was having dinner with. "The Seattle library? That opened, what—six years ago, Michael. We did a piece on it six years ago."

"I thought maybe an update. It's been here a while, people's opinions on it have changed, the materials inside are starting to wear. The chairs are all made of rubberized foam, but the surfaces are starting to crack. Maybe something about materials, I thought."

"That's pretty technical for us. And we're trying to do less technical stuff these days, not more."

"Okay," Michael said. He didn't know how to do this. How did one do this? "The thing is, Lucas? I need to sell something. I need to write and sell something."

"Dry spell, huh?"

"Yeah, a dry spell. And my wife and I have split up, so—"

"You and Cathy are splitting up? Cathy is your wife's name, right?"

"Yes. We're not together anymore."

"Shit. I'm sorry to hear about that. How long?"

"Almost a year now, actually. It's fine. But we're doing the formal stuff now, so of course I've got legal fees. And I still haven't been able to find a full time thing. And Cathy and I are arguing over custody stuff, and the bills are kind of stacking up."

"Why are you in Seattle, again? You guys are still living in Denver, right?"

"Yes. I just hadn't ever been here, to Seattle, and there was a cheap deal, a promotion thing. And my son is with Cathy for a few days, so it seemed like an opportunity. I borrowed some money to get here and look around." Before this conversation, these things had made perfect sense to him. Now, saying them aloud to Lucas, he sensed gaps of logic. "I just felt like I needed to do something. I needed to look at something and write about it. It's been five months since I've placed anything. No one's taking anything."

"You can say that again. No one's buying any magazines, either."

"I know, but Lucas, I need money. I need *work*. I need to be able to show the lawyers that I can pay bills and be a parent. Any kind of paying piece right now would be fine. Just something."

"Shit, Michael. The magazine here is drowning, too. I'd give you an assignment, but I don't have any assignment to give out right now. Half of the last issue was written by the interns."

I shouldn't have been honest, he thought. What was that inane saying? *Nothing succeeds like success*. I should have called and acted as if incredible things were happening for me, and *then* asked if Lucas wanted anything. Too late now. "Okay," Michael said. "I understand. But I'm in Seattle tonight and tomorrow night. What would you suggest I do, as long as I'm here?"

Lucas sighed, and then spoke in a lowered voice, as if passing along a secret. "I would suggest you do what the hardcore freelancers do, Michael: find something. No, find *five* things, and write them all."

"And can I come back to you with my five things? Can I send them to you to look over?"

"Sure, but Michael, listen: no guarantees. We don't have money here, either."

"That's fine. I'll find something good."

"And listen, if you're really freelancing, then don't just do architecture. Write about food. Write about travel. Write an essay about your feelings. Things *women* like, Michael. That's where the money is. Not in architecture."

"Okay."

"You're a talented writer and I wish I could do more for you, but all I can promise is that I'll look at things. If you need me to pass stuff to the right people at other places, I'm happy to do that, too."

"Thanks, Lucas."

After he hung up, Michael looked at his computer screen. There were five words typed at the top of an otherwise blank page: *Library Article, by Michael Novak*. After considering for a moment, he deleted the first two words. Then he closed the screen.

The reflection of himself in the doors wobbled as the elevator descended, and he felt his knees compress as the car decelerated and shuddered to a stop. A bright-sounding bell announced the opening of the doors, and he stepped into a lobby whose neutral-shade walls and furnishings seemed careful variations on some ur-taupe not actually present, but referred to everywhere. A concierge stood behind an oak lectern near the doors, thoughtfully chewing his lip, and Michael couldn't help but note that the man was roughly his own age, if not a bit older. "Can I offer you any directions this evening, sir?" the man asked.

"I was just about to head out to dinner. Do you have any suggestions?"

"Of course," the concierge said, conveying an alert and elegant intelligence despite the navy-blazer-and-red-tie uniform that suggested the staff had recently arrived from an East Coast prep school. "What kind of place are you looking for? Are you meeting someone?"

"No, I'm alone. But a view of the water would be nice, if it's not exorbitantly expensive."

"It doesn't have to be," the man said. "Any particular cuisine?"

"No. I'd like a good drink before dinner, though."

"There's a restaurant called Place Pigalle that might work for that. It's too late for you to get a reservation, but it's early enough that they could probably slip you in at the bar."

"You're the second person who's recommended them," Michael said. "Are they running some kind of promotion with the citizens here?"

The concierge smiled politely as he circled a spot on a photocopied map of downtown. "No. It's just a place with a view that doesn't have to be expensive." He drew a careful line from the hotel to the spot he had circled, and handed the map to Michael. "It's not hard to find."

On the way to the restaurant, Michael stopped in a convenience store and bought a pack of cigarettes. It was a habit he'd quit years ago but had picked up again recently, probably in no small part for the perverse pleasure to be found in spending money he didn't have on something that was bad for him. When he exited the store and lit a cigarette, rain was falling in fat, widely-spaced drops. He'd forgotten his umbrella, but it was only the timid or vain-looking pedestrians who were using theirs, and he felt a sense of satisfaction in the dampness that formed on the shoulders and back of his jacket.

Sofie had told him Place Pigalle was small, but it turned out to be even smaller than he'd expected—just eight white-linen-covered tables on a black and white tile floor, and a short bar along the far side of the room. The oak walls and their decorative moldings exhibited the dull sheen of decades of wear. Lilies rose from small vases at the center of each table, willow branches rose from a ceramic urn in the corner, and three large windows at the back offered a view of the bay: a few striated clouds hung near the horizon, but the sky seemed to be clearing as the sun descended. The hostess showed Michael to a seat at the bar, where he ordered a Manhattan, drank it too quickly to appreciate, and ordered another. Sitting with his back to the room and the view, he ate every piece of bread on the small plate before him, and then a plate of oysters on the half shell. The bartender, a friendly young guy with a tattoo of a Chinese character on his forearm, asked Michael whether he was in town on business or pleasure. "It's unclear," Michael said, and they both laughed. The bartender had just placed Michael's dinner of braised lamb and a glass of red wine in front of him when someone touched his elbow.

He turned to find Sofie standing there, a quizzical look on her face. "You're here," she said.

"It was recommended," he said.

"You're feeling better, then?"

"Much. I slept. And now I'm eating." He raised his glass. "Drinking helps, too."

"I'm happy to see that. I thought you were going to pass out today."

"No—though that might have been easier. But inconvenient to you."

"It would have been a first."

"The wrong kind. But could we pick up the tour again tomorrow? If I promise I'll be in good health?"

She smiled. "We already talked about that, before you left. You said you were going to call."

"I don't remember that. I'm sorry. What time is good for you? I have the whole day."

She glanced across the room, and Michael followed her gaze to a table for two, where the man Sofie had shared a laugh with earlier in the day was studying the menu. "How about ten?" she said.

"Perfect."

"I'll let you eat that lamb now. I should join my friend," she said, nodding toward his plate as she touched him on the arm and then walked across the room to her waiting companion.

The last rays of the setting sun struck the wall behind the bar, and the bartender disappeared during the few minutes they burned with blinding brightness. When they faded, he and the other servers reappeared, lighting candles on the bar and at the tables as the sun disappeared behind the dusky blue rise of land that was Bainbridge

Island. Michael feigned a distracted gaze out the windows while stealing a few glances at Sofie and the man from the library. The man was speaking with great enthusiasm, gesturing with the zeal of a symphony conductor—when it glinted in the candlelight, Michael noticed a wedding ring on the man's hand. Sofie listened, nodding occasionally, but also allowing her gaze to wander from the half-eaten piece of salmon on her plate to the view out the windows, and then to the surrounding diners. Her eyes met Michael's for a fraction of a second, but she betrayed no recognition, her focus moving past in an unbroken sweep before returning to the man across the table from her in time for her to nod encouragingly to him.

Later, Michael was drinking a cup of after-dinner coffee and making conversation with the bartender about the Seahawks when he realized Sofie's date was standing next to him. "Hello," the man said. "I'm Robert. We traded e-mail when you were scheduling your tour of the library. Sofie told me you're going to try again tomorrow."

"Yes, I wasn't feeling well earlier. But I'm better now."

"Please," Robert said, gesturing toward his table. "Join us for dessert."

"I couldn't."

"I insist. I've been wanting to meet you. And there's no reason to sit alone at the bar."

So he followed Robert across the room and, taking a seat at their table, said hello to Sofie. She smiled and nodded, but said nothing.

"It's always an honor to have a critic of your stature visit the library," Robert said.

Michael couldn't tell if Robert's overvaluation of him was the result of formal politeness, or if the man was mocking him. "I don't recall being of any particular stature," he said. "And neither am I a critic anymore."

"Oh, yes. Sofie said something about that paper being one of the ones that went under. It's too bad. But if you're no longer a critic, what are you now? You must be up to something."

"Not much."

"I'm sure that will be temporary. Sofie says you're not writing about the library, but I was wondering if you might at least tell us what you think."

What he thought? What he thought could take up the rest of the evening. "I like it," he said.

'That's all?"

"What more is there to say?"

Robert settled into his chair, displeased. "You're holding out. You were much more detailed in your analysis of the Trade Center site."

Michael looked at Sofie. "It's odd how one old newspaper article of no real importance is going around here."

"I thought it was interesting," Robert said.

Michael was confident it was not. And he still couldn't pin down the intention behind Robert's tone. "You're being polite."

"I'm serious. I would like to have read more, but I guess the newspaper's articles are no longer online. In the Trade Center article, though, you alluded to opportunities that weren't taken. 'A healing solution,' I think you called it. I just wonder what you meant by that."

Michael looked to Sofie again, but she returned his look with the same absence of expression she had worn when first introducing herself that morning. She seemed bored. "I feel like I wrote that article a hundred years ago," Michael said. "There was a window of time in which people cared about the World Trade Center site, but having had strong personal feelings about it strikes me as odd now. I don't live there, and I only have a dim memory of that article. It was vanity."

"You're being shy," Robert said. "I'm sure you remember what you meant by a 'healing solution.'"

"I do remember having the conversation we're having right now," Michael said, "but with other people, six or seven years ago. I know where it goes—you want to know what I would have done if I were an actual architect, and not just a critic."

"Yes."

There was no good reason for them to be discussing the World Trade Center site while sitting in Seattle years after all of the decisions had been made—it just happened to be the only article of his still floating around on the Internet. He also felt that Robert was purposely drawing him out for reasons that had nothing to do with the World Trade Center. Though he had spent only a few minutes with him, Robert's insistent manner, and the way he spoke, gestured, and held himself now left Michael confident that Robert was the kind of man who held a grudge against society and everyone in it, because society had failed to grant him the degree of power and influence he felt he deserved. Michael recognized this attitude, and understood immediately and confidently that Robert was this type of man, because Michael, too, was this type of man. And knew it. He was competitive, but frustrated—wanting to dispute, but needing to cloak his aggression. This was why it was possible to dislike and respect someone at the same time.

He disliked Robert but, so far, respected him. And it was those same contradictory feelings, Michael believed, that were responsible for Robert's formal tone.

He thought: So then what do I care?

"I like transformation," he said. "From violence to beauty. I thought it would be nice to create a memorial that recognized the scope of the event. There are maps that show how far the clouds of debris traveled. At the time, I thought it would be powerful to create something that incorporated every building that had been touched by that debris."

"But wouldn't that be the majority of Manhattan?"

He's never left the West Coast, Michael thought. "No, just Lower Manhattan, and not even all of it. But every building touched by the debris could have a glass exterior, for instance, or some other type of cladding. You could even adjust the degree of each structure's involvement, from an entire façade on significantly hit buildings to just a small piece or gesture on some of the last-touched buildings. You'd be able to see endless lines of whatever material you chose in those streets near the towers, but when you saw a small bit of the same material on a building farther uptown, you would get a sense of the spatial extent of the disaster. It would have nothing to do with building some kind of huge new powerful megatower, and everything to do with memory."

Robert nodded indulgently, as if Michael were a good, but very young, student. "It's an interesting idea," he said. "But impossible, right? You would have to persuade every building owner to give up control over the appearance of their buildings."

"There might be room for interpretation. I like to think that if everyone understood the project, they might *want* to take part."

"That's a generous view of people. You're an idealist—a dreamer. I love it."

"My idea, or your description of me as a dreamer?"

Robert laughed. "It's the same thing, isn't it?"

Michael felt like he, too, was on the verge of laughing. He wasn't sure if it was because his idea was ridiculous, though, or because the fact that he was sitting there explaining it to Robert and Sofie was more so. He understood Robert had scored some kind of victory over him, but didn't particularly care. He had played along willingly. "I should go," he said. "Thank you for chatting."

"You're welcome to stay. You haven't had any dessert," Robert said.

"No, thank you. But Sofie—tomorrow morning at ten?"

"Yes," she said. "Have a nice evening, Michael."

After paying his bill, he embarked on a walk around downtown, his thoughts unreeling in a way that had become familiar to him over the last few weeks. Some part of his mind seemed involved in a search of moments and images from his childhood, as if the mental agency or drive behind the process had determined that the object of its search lay within his earliest years. That evening, as he walked up and down a few streets, he found himself remembering walking downstairs, after the service was over, and into the basement of the Catholic church his family had attended in the small town he'd grown up in. The crush of men in their ties and women in their blouses, the smell of perfume and cologne mingling in the crowded, low-ceilinged stairwell, the scores of shuffling feet: it had been years since he'd thought about post-Mass coffee and doughnuts in the church basement. So why was his mind replaying it now? If I don't understand what my own mind is doing, he thought, then what chance do I have? Unable to find an answer to that question, and after walking aimlessly for he knew not how long, he looked up to find himself in front of his hotel, and when he stepped through the front door, he found the same concierge still at his post. "Was the restaurant what you were hoping for, sir?" he asked.

"How long have you worked here?" Michael asked.

"A little over a year."

"What did you do before that?"

"I was a programmer. I wrote code, for software."

"Microsoft?"

"No. A small company. It went out of business."

"But is your code still out there? In any software people use, or on the Internet?"

The man laughed. "Oh, God no. Or I hope not. We never even got to de-bugging it. We never finished the product."

"Well, the restaurant was perfect," Michael said. "Thank you very much."

"I'm glad to hear that," the man said. "You're welcome."

When Michael made it to his room, he opened his laptop and checked his e-mail. Amid various junk e-mails, there was one from his wife. He opened it to find that it consisted of one word: *Nice.*

"And this is the Books Spiral," Sofie said the next morning. "Designed to allow patrons to move continuously from zero to one thousand in the Dewey decimal system." She walked more slowly than the previous day, and remained alongside him rather than leading. This was possibly because upon entering the Spiral, leading was no longer necessary. One simply followed the numbers.

"He planned this spiral years before this building," Michael said. "For some other building or competition." They walked the slightly inclined path of black rubber tiles with white numbers indicating where they were in the system. The walls were glass: to the Spiral's exterior, clear glass that allowed a view of the rooms of shelves and books, and to its interior, opaque yellow glass, brightly lit. "What a thing," he said, "to have an idea, but to be prevented from acting on it. So you hold it for years, waiting for a chance."

Sofie's hair was in even more elaborate pinned braids today, and she wore grey wool slacks and a ribbed black sweater. Michael wore khaki slacks and a black dress shirt. He wondered, because he had dressed less formally with her in mind, if Sofie had dressed more formally with him in mind.

Stepping through a gap in the glass wall and into a row of bookshelves, he pulled a title from a shelf, opened it a moment, and then returned it to its place.

"Checking to see if they're real?" Sofie said.

"Yes," he said. "It's an interesting choice, going with real books."

"Expensive," she said.

They stepped out of the room and returned to the path. Looking down at the black rubber tiles instead of at him, Sofie said, "Why aren't you planning on writing anything about the building?"

"Because I'm not employed to do that anymore," he said.

"But couldn't you sell it to someone? If you went ahead and wrote something?"

Michael watched two women, one middle-aged and the other elderly, come around the corner. They were headed downward, and the older woman's arm was linked in the younger's for support. The two couples—the older and younger woman, and Michael and Sofie—nodded politely as they passed. After the women had moved further down the path, Sofie said, "You're not like I expected you."

"What did you expect?"

"From the tone of your writing, I expected someone arrogant. No offense."

"None taken. I am arrogant."

"Maybe in print. But you don't seem like it in real life."

"Is it okay if I think it's funny that you drew this conclusion from an old story in a defunct newspaper? No one gets, or got, their architecture criticism from the *Rocky Mountain News*. The fact that they even employed an architecture writer as long as they did was amazing, and that decision was probably one of many similar ones they made that led them out of business."

"They had to pay some kind of writers. Isn't it just the Internet that put them out of business? No matter what kind of writers they were paying?"

"Other newspapers put them out of business. When you can get the *New York Times* free online, why get the *Rocky Mountain News*? You don't. But you're right, having been fired isn't why I'm not writing. The whole ship-going-down moment probably gave all of us who worked there more attention than we've ever had, for a brief window of time. I had a bunch of strange offers from a number of websites or odd little magazines. A few of them were leftist things that had made their own assumptions about me based on some other things I'd written, I guess—little angry and desperate magazines that I kind of admired, when I looked at them. But then one asked if I would write a manifesto for post-colonial architecture, and another wanted an essay about the 'architecture of resistance.' There was even one that suggested I write about feminist architecture. I wasn't even sure what they meant, but I could have had plenty of writing to do, if I'd accepted all of the offers."

They followed The Spiral around one of its turns and continued upward. Patrons moved past in either direction, some descending, others climbing more rapidly than Michael and Sofie, impatient to reach the top.

"But you didn't take any of them up?"

"There wasn't real money involved. And my marriage was breaking up, and not gracefully, so it was easy just to say no. And I maybe don't want to write any more articles in which I criticize people from some lofty theoretical height."

"What would you rather do?"

"I'd like to do something with more immediate and dramatic effects."

"In writing, or in life?"

He smiled. "Sofie, I probably just want revenge."

"Against who?"

"Everyone. I'm aware that when people lose their jobs or marriages, they go through these feelings. I'm highly aware of it, because I've read many, many articles about it. And yet I can't stop myself from going through them, too, and I've been circling around in them for a couple years now. The era for architecture critics employed by newspapers is over, so I think I should become someone else. And if I want to remake myself, I should choose something I love. And then I think that, unfortunately, I love writing about buildings. So maybe I should start a website, or just start writing about architecture even more than before, and try to become one of the very few voices that gets hired by one of the very few newspapers or magazines that do employ people like me. And yet writing about architecture *even more* is exactly the thing that has earned me no money for the last two years, and the definition of insanity is doing the same thing over and over but expecting different results, *et cetera*. I have been told this, and I have told myself this. I have a son who's about to turn five, and when he asks me questions about the world, or how to be and act, or when he just needs my influence on those things, there's a weird part of me that's no longer confident in telling him about the world. I try to hide it from him, but kids pick up on things. Aside from an occasional freelance piece I don't care much about, and one online thing that flamed out in a month, I've been unemployed for almost two years. So what should I tell him about the world?"

"I think kids are okay with honesty. Aren't they?"

"But I don't want him to know the truth. His dad has been incredibly stubborn about doing a certain thing and living a certain way, and it looks like his dad was wrong. But won't admit it."

"He can understand why a newspaper might go out of business, though, can't he?"

"Maybe. But should I explain that in the last few months at the paper, my editor, who had been a friend of mine for ten years, may have hidden a job opportunity from me so he could take it himself? But that the opportunity has essentially turned into a vapid Japanese-toy-and-witty-T-shirt lifestyle magazine that's really just glorified advertising, so I should be glad that he didn't pass along the job offer, because the job has essentially ended his life as a useful thinker and person?"

Sofie laughed. "That's the arrogance I was expecting," she said.

"You're happy now?"

"You need a sacrificial victim."

"The problem is that I dislike violence. And also, to be honest, it strikes me as insufficient."

"You want something more than violence?"

"More effective than violence."

"You mean more destructive than violence."

"If you want to make an omelette," he said, "you have to break a few eggs."

"Stalin said that."

"He did? How do you know that?"

"What do you mean? I know things. From reading. The world. That's who said that. It's just common knowledge."

"It wasn't common knowledge to me. I must have missed that day."

"I didn't mean it that way," she said. "I'm just—" She gestured hopelessly in the air before her, but then shrugged, defeated. "I didn't mean it the way it sounded. It's not like I think everyone should know that."

"You worry about whether you're being nice to people, don't you?"

"Doesn't everyone?"

He laughed. "No. Not everyone does."

They stepped from the last black rubber panel of the Spiral and into a vast carpeted floor. "This is the Reading Room," she said. The floor was filled with more groups of molded foam chairs—royal blue here—and the glass walls rose inward to where they converged with the glass roof, so that the entire floor was flooded with natural light. Michael walked to a balcony where the walls rose just beyond reach. Mist beaded in crystalline drops on the outside of the diamond-shaped windows, and he saw, close up, the fine aluminum mesh that was undetectable from a distance, but which was embedded within the glass panels to break up and soften entering light. "The mesh had to be designed by OMA and manufactured specifically for the library, because no one had used anything like it before," Sofie said.

"Architectural courtesy," Michael said. He leaned over the railing and looked down. A small gap along the side of the building allowed him a view of multiple lower balconies and, at the bottom, a thin section of the lobby floor. He looked up through the ceiling into the gray sky, and then scanned the faces of the people in the Reading Room. Some sat in the chairs, but others were milling about, gazing up into the sky as he had.

"Are you looking for someone?" Sofie asked.

"What?"

"When you look around, it's like you're expecting to see someone. Like you're on the lookout."

"I've just been tired lately. And maybe a little anxious."

"Is that what happened yesterday? An anxiety attack?"

He turned and faced her, as if to show that even if she had seen him looking anxious, he was also capable of confidence. "You're very persistent," he said.

"Maybe. I'm sorry if I shouldn't have asked."

"No," he said. "It's admirable. Some questions are just tougher than others."

"What do you mean? You don't know if you're looking for someone, or you don't know if you're having anxiety attacks?"

He looked at her, at the twists of green and brown and gold in her eyes, at the slope of her small nose, at her beaded earrings and the wisps of hair that escaped her braids. "The man you went to dinner with last night is married," he said. "But not to you."

Her face clouded—quicker and more severely than he had expected. "There's nothing wrong with going to dinner with a co-worker," she said. "I'm sorry that he criticized your idea, if that's what you're getting at. He's a friend of mine."

"I'm sure he is, but Place Pigalle didn't strike me as casual dining. And the two of you don't work for a business, so I doubt it was a business dinner."

Sofie looked around the room as if checking to see who might be listening.

"Now you're the one scanning the room," he said. "I don't care about my idea. My idea is stupid. All I'm saying is that anyone in that restaurant could tell that something's going on between the two of you. I'm about two years down the road from that game, and I understand that there are various ways you can talk about what you're doing, and that's fine. Or am I entirely mistaken?"

She shook her head as if confused. "How did we get here? I guess I got personal first."

"I don't mind. But I can be persistent, too."

"About my personal life?"

"If that's what we're talking about, yes."

"You didn't answer my question about what you're scared of, though. So I won't answer yours."

"Who said I was scared of something?"

"It looked like fear."

"You wouldn't tell me how old you were, either, so this is

par for the course. I don't understand why you think you're allowed to ask me so many questions, but I can't ask you anything back. You're pretty aggressive for someone who supposedly cares about whether she's being nice."

"I'm sorry," she said with exaggerated nonchalance. "The tour is over, really. This is the top floor. I know you said you're not going to write about the building, but I left a media packet at the info desk for you anyway, just in case. You can pick it up on the way out. From Robert."

"Thank you."

She turned to face him, and they traded the same look they had already traded a number of times that day. Michael again felt the frightening sense of there not being enough distance between them.

"I do care what you think of me," Sofie said. "But I don't know why. I think it's a weakness."

"If that's true, you're definitely getting stronger."

She nodded slowly, as if disappointed. "I hope you enjoyed the building," she said. "I'm sorry I couldn't be of more help." She walked away in the direction of the elevators that would return her to the lobby. He watched her, hoping she would look back, but she didn't. So he sat alone in one of the reading chairs, watching patrons and tourists continue to mill around the room—looking up, looking down, trying to make sense of it.

There's nothing to make sense of, he thought.

He did not pick up his media packet. He returned to the lobby of the library via the stairwell, walked out the door, across the street, and back to his hotel room, where he immediately felt restless. He felt he had behaved badly with Sofie, had hurt her unnecessarily, and he was unhappy with himself. It was not simply an apology he felt he owed her, but something more, and he felt this need as a charge that left him disturbed. He sat on the edge of the bed, his fingers on his temples as he stared at the carpet and tried to decide what to do, or if there was even anything that could be done. It was not so much that he needed to say anything, he decided—saying things had gotten him in enough trouble—but that he wanted just to see her once more. He felt that if he could look her in the eye once more, she might at least see that he was not a malevolent person. He was not who he had been in his last conversation with her.

He went to the window and looked down at the library. You are a cliché, he thought.

His room phone rang, the loudness of it startling him.

"I'm not happy with the way our conversation ended," she said when he answered.

"Yes," Sofie said. "The man I was with last night is married. And yes, we like each other. Are you judging me?"

Though it was growing late, Place Pigalle was still busy. The room was filled with loud conversation, and the big windows stood like three dark rectangles on the west wall—three frames of the night. After agreeing to meet Sofie here in the evening, Michael had spent the morning at the art museum, and the afternoon visiting various tourist destinations downtown. He had eaten small, inexpensive meals at restaurants listed as being good. He'd taken the monorail to Frank Gehry's rock and roll building, walked once around the exterior, and took the monorail right back to where he'd started, taking notes the whole time. He had typed up his notes, as well as every thought and impression he could remember from the entire two days he'd been there. When he was done, he read them over. It was disappointing, reading his thoughts—they hadn't the slightest thing to do with architecture. He had been happy when the time arrived for him to close his computer and walk to the restaurant. It was late in the evening, and though there were still diners at the tables, he and Sofie were the only people at the bar. "I'm not judging you," he said. "You just didn't seem happy."

"It's my job to be happy?"

He shrugged.

"I've been told I don't smile enough," she said. "A number of times in my life random men walking past me on the street have said, 'Smile!' Like it's a command. Fake happiness is compulsory."

"I'm sorry."

She glared at him for a moment, as if he were one of the men who had told her to smile, but then looked out the windows and into the night. "But you're right. That's why I'm leaving."

"Where are you going?"

"I don't know. Somewhere else. Some other city."

"When?"

"Next week. Tomorrow. Tonight. I don't know. I should give two weeks notice. But in the two weeks I'll change my mind a hundred times."

"I did that."

"Changed your mind?"

"Left. My wife."

"How old did you say your son was?"

"Almost five."

"How often do you see him?"

"Two nights a week. I want it to be more. We're arguing about that."

"So why did you come to Seattle if you're not going to write about the building?"

"I'm trying to kickstart myself. I need to see things if I want to figure out a way to say things. And I'm worried that I'm slipping toward becoming someone who doesn't say anything anymore."

"So you do want to write something."

"I just don't have an assignment. I don't have a job."

"And you're having a mid-life crisis."

"I didn't choose it. The newspaper went out of business."

"But you did choose the marriage crisis. It sounded to me like you caused it."

"There's no reason to argue about that. But what I feel like is that I'm trying to keep from being crushed by something. Something not me."

"What kind of thing?"

"I don't know. Or I think I know, but I don't know how to say it. Or I think I could say it, but it would sound crazy. And maybe it would be crazy."

"What would you say?"

"I don't want to start," he said. "Because if I start, I feel like I'll have to talk for hours, and it would just be a lot of anger, and I'd attack everyone I've ever known and everything that's ever happened, but I would also, by going over everything that has ever happened to me and has ever happened to them, be trying to say something about how I actually loved them, but it was just wrong, it just doesn't work, for no reason. But I don't want to start. I don't want to do that with you."

"But what if you wrote that kind of thing? Could you write about it?"

"I don't write things like that. I write architecture criticism. I have an advanced degree in architectural theory, and that's what I'm good at writing. That's it."

She grabbed a fresh cocktail napkin from a stack on the bartender's side of the counter and placed it in front of him. "Here," she said. "Write only what fits on this napkin." She pulled a blue ballpoint pen from her purse and placed it on the napkin. "Whatever you want, it doesn't matter. Just the simplest thing."

He picked up the pen and looked at the blank white napkin, and then again at her. Then he wrote: *I'm 41 years old. How old are you?*

"Thirty," she said.

I may have missed my chance to do something, he wrote.

"I don't think so."

He looked in her eyes again, and she looked back, unblinking. A waitress slipped past behind them carrying a tray of precariously balanced entrees.

I keep thinking about your eyes, he wrote.

She looked at the sentence and, without moving her eyes from it, said very quietly, as if he had spoken aloud and someone might have heard, "I understand."

I've only known you two days.

She nodded.

Do you want to go somewhere with me?

She closed her eyes and sat, motionless. When she opened them again she was no longer looking at the napkin, but instead at the section of bar in front of her. She began breathing rapidly.

"Don't answer that," he said. "I'm sorry."

She glanced at him, and then turned again to the window and shook her head as if she were struggling to speak, but couldn't.

"I wish I hadn't written that," he said.

"It's okay," she said. "I just—I have to leave."

"I'm sorry."

"Not right now. It's okay. I just have to leave this city. I have to go somewhere new. It doesn't matter where."

"It matters where."

"Where should I go?"

"Somewhere big."

"I keep thinking about a farm. Somewhere in the country."

"You'll be alone with yourself."

"It's other people. My attachments are messed up. I need isolation."

"A big city distracts you from yourself. It's a better kind of isolation. On a farm you'd follow yourself around constantly."

"You've lived on a farm?"

"Never," he said. "That's why I'm so confident about what it's like. I should stop talking."

When the bartender asked them if they needed anything, Sofie didn't acknowledge the man's presence. Michael told him they were fine, and when the man had moved off and left them alone again, she put the tips of her fingers over his and pressed down, briefly, before curling them into a fist that she set on the bar in front of her, as if her hand were an object rather than a part of her. She looked at him and smiled. "I need to go home," she said. She stood, opened her purse, and pulled out a wallet.

"No," he said. "I'll get it."

"Okay." She stood there for a moment, nodding. "I have

to leave," she repeated, though in a tone that suggested she was speaking to herself rather than to him. But it worked: she turned, threaded her way deftly through the tables, and disappeared out the door.

He found her headed downhill, toward the water, and began walking calmly but quickly after her. Eventually, she turned back and saw him. "Are you following me?" she called back over her shoulder.

"Are you trying to get away from me?" he said. "I feel like I shouldn't let you out of my sight."

"So you are following me."

"I thought we were walking together."

She darted across the street, against the light. Michael waited for a car to pass, and then crossed after her. There was nowhere downhill left for her to go, and she stopped, leaning against the high wall that overlooked the shore thirty feet below. Michael could hear the waves rolling against the jumbled concrete rocks, and heard Sofie laughing as he walked toward her.

"You just want to sleep with me," she said. "That's all. You want to fuck me and then get on your plane tomorrow."

"No," he said. "It's more than that."

"It's nothing more than that," she said. "Some things haven't gone well for you and now you're moping and you want someone to make you feel better. Maybe you deserved it. It sounds like you did."

He looked at her without moving.

"Don't look at me that way," she said tiredly.

"What way?"

"Like an animal, waiting. Like you want a fight."

He walked a few steps down the sidewalk as if leaving, then turned and came back. "What do you want with me?"

"What do you mean?"

"I don't want to follow you. I can get you a cab, if you want. But *you* called *me*. You said you wanted to talk tonight. What do you want me to do?"

"I don't know."

"Do you want me, too?"

"Why is that what everything is about? Everybody wants to fuck everybody."

"You're not very good at cursing."

"But it's true."

"You're right. You need to get out of here. Out of this city."

"Now you're telling me what to do?"

"I'm agreeing with you."

"I didn't ask for your advice."

"You're better than that guy."

She shook her head. "Shut up," she said.

"He doesn't deserve you."

"And I suppose you do? You just want to sleep with me. That's all."

"I want that," he said. "But I want something more, too."

She leaned out over the wall and screamed. The sound traveled out into the breeze and died in the heavy night air. A few people turned their heads, but Sofie was smiling, and Michael was standing apart from her, and it wasn't an area in which people got involved in other people's business late at night. Sofie peered down into the darkness below, as if gauging the distance. "I should jump," she said. "I always feel like jumping."

"Kant said the body wants to try things, regardless of whether they're a good idea. But we stop the body."

"You men and your theories. If I jumped, you'd run and grab someone so you could explain why I did it."

"You're not going to jump."

"You're right. I never do." She walked past him in the direction of the street, and he turned to watch her gesture toward the driver of a cab that was letting a couple out at the curb.

"Where are you going?" he called to her.

She ducked into the cab and pulled the door shut. He was walking toward it when it pulled away from the curb and into traffic. He watched the taillights for a bit, but then they merged with so many other lights—traffic and stores, bars and streetlights—that he lost them.

When he emerged from the shower the next morning, he noticed the orange message light flashing on his room's telephone. He picked it up, hoping maybe it was a message from Sofie, but it turned out to be an automated message telling him when check-out time was, and his options for paying. There were no other messages.

His flight was in a couple hours. He dressed, went down to the street, and walked around the library once more. It wasn't open, though, and he knew his hope that he might find her there was just magical thinking. The building stood in silence, shining in the sunlight of the clear day. From the street level, it looked like a smashed box. Glass and steel hung dramatically over the sidewalk. He walked once around the block to study its faces. Each face differed markedly from its siblings, but all four spoke the same language of steel and glass. He lingered on the street. There was an energy there. Even the people out on the street seemed more alert on this block, some walking past with their faces upturned, studying the anomalous structure. One of them, a young man with piercings in his ears, nose, and lips, said as he walked past Michael, "It's fucked up, isn't it?"

Michael nodded. It was time for him to gather his things and catch a bus to the airport. He stopped for a moment, though, to look up beyond the building, to the sky behind it. The other subject Michael had caught his mind studying recently—after childhood memories, after marriage and career slights—was the sky. He had caught himself staring up into it on days like today, when it was huge and blue and empty, and felt he was getting better at telling the difference between some of the sky's blues. There was the burnished blue that presented a sense of liquid depth, a sky one could fall into. There was also the pale flat blue that sometimes appeared on early afternoons, a wall of sky he couldn't help but feel would do violence to the planes heading toward it. There was the blue-green morning sky that seemed like a dome placed over the world, the gray-blue sky that lay overhead like a painted ceiling, and the violet-blue evening sky that hung like the skin of an immense fruit. Finally, there was the white-blue sky of the hottest days—a sky that seemed an absence of sky, with a blue that was an absence of blue. That was what the sky looked like to him when he looked up past the library, and it was this sky that he liked best, because it felt the most true. Because, as Michael knew anyone familiar with the atmosphere could tell him, the sky isn't actually blue. Because it isn't actually there.

ACKNOWLEDGMENTS

Jodee Stanley, Frances Badgett, Jeff McMahon, Holly MacArthur, Lee Montgomery, Cheston Knapp, Michelle Wildgen, Tonaya Thompson, Deah Paulson, Kevin Sampsell, Allison Lorentzen, Charles D'Ambrosio, Mary Rechner, Evan Schneider, Jennifer Ruth, John Smyth, A.B. Paulson, Jesse Lichtenstein, Jon Raymond, Dan Frazier, Heather Larimer, Camela Raymond, Laura Moulton, Kathleen Holt, Apricot Irving, Jamie Passaro, Scott McEachern, Robin Romm, Erika Recordon, Peyton Marshall, Paul Martone, Michael Heald, Holly Laycock, Benjamin Craig, Lucas Bernhardt, Rachel Greben, and others who read, responded, encouraged: thank you.